TRIANGLE OF POWER

Borgo Press Books by JOHN RUSSELL FEARN

1,000-Year Voyage: A Science Fiction Novel * *Anjani the Mighty: A Lost Race Novel* (Anjani #2) * *Black Maria, M.A.: A Classic Crime Novel* (Black Maria #1) * *The Crimson Rambler: A Crime Novel* * *Don't Touch Me: A Crime Novel* * *Dynasty of the Small: Classic Science Fiction Stories* * *The Empty Coffins: A Mystery of Horror* * *The Fourth Door: A Mystery Novel* * *From Afar: A Science Fiction Mystery* * *Fugitive of Time: A Classic Science Fiction Novel* * *The G-Bomb: A Science Fiction Novel* * *The Genial Dinosaur* (Herbert the Dinosaur #2) * *The Gold of Akada: A Jungle Adventure Novel* (Anjani #1) * *Here and Now: A Science Fiction Novel* * *Into the Unknown: A Science Fiction Tale* * *Last Conflict: Classic Science Fiction Stories* * *Legacy from Sirius: A Classic Science Fiction Novel* * *The Man from Hell: Classic Science Fiction Stories* * *The Man Who Was Not: A Crime Novel* * *Manton's World: A Classic Science Fiction Novel* * *Moon Magic: A Novel of Romance* (as Elizabeth Rutland) * *The Murdered Schoolgirl: A Classic Crime Novel* (Black Maria #2) * *One Remained Seated: A Classic Crime Novel* (Black Maria #3) * *One Way Out: A Crime Novel* (with Philip Harbottle) * *Pattern of Murder: A Classic Crime Novel* * *Reflected Glory: A Dr. Castle Classic Crime Novel* * *Robbery Without Violence: Two Science Fiction Crime Stories* * *Rule of the Brains: Classic Science Fiction Stories* * *Shattering Glass: A Crime Novel* * *The Silvered Cage: A Scientific Murder Mystery* * *Slaves of Ijax: A Science Fiction Novel* * *Something from Mercury: Classic Science Fiction Stories* * *The Space Warp: A Science Fiction Novel* * *A Thing of the Past* (Herbert the Dinosaur #1) * *Thy Arm Alone: A Classic Crime Novel* (Black Maria #4) * *The Time Trap: A Science Fiction Novel* * *Vision Sinister: A Scientific Detective Thriller* * *Voice of the Conqueror: A Classic Science Fiction Novel* * *What Happened to Hammond? A Scientific Mystery* * *Within That Room!: A Classic Crime Novel*

THE GOLDEN AMAZON SAGA

1. *World Beneath Ice* * 2. *Lord of Atlantis* * 3. *Triangle of Power* * 4. *The Amethyst City* * 5. *Daughter of the Amazon* * 6. *Quorne Returns* * 7. *The Central Intelligence* * 8. *The Cosmic Crusaders* * 9. *Parasite Planet* * 10. *World Out of Step* * 11. *The Shadow People* * 12. *Kingpin Planet* * 13. *World in Reverse* * 14. *Dwellers in Darkness* * 15. *World in Duplicate* * 16. *Lords of Creation* * 17. *Duel with Colossus* * 18. *Standstill Planet* * 19. *Ghost World* * 20. *Earth Divided* * 21. *Chameleon Planet* (with Philip Harbottle)

TRIANGLE OF POWER

THE GOLDEN AMAZON SAGA, BOOK THREE

JOHN RUSSELL FEARN

Edited by Philip Harbottle

THE BORGO PRESS

MMXII

TRIANGLE OF POWER

FIRST BORGO PRESS EDITION

Published by Wildside Press LLC

www.wildsidebooks.com

DEDICATION

To the Memory of Ken Slater

Contents

THE GOLDEN AMAZON
by Philip Harbottle

In 1943 British writer John Russell Fearn decided to quit writing for the American pulp science fiction magazines, and to concentrate instead on books for the English market. Within a very few years he became established as a leading novelist in several genres, not only science fiction, but also mystery and detective fiction, and westerns.

His first new SF novel, *The Golden Amazon*, was published by World's Work in April 1944. In this story, a little girl of three years of age is made the subject of an idealistic scientist's illegal glandular experiments. The scientist's dream is to end world wars by creating a woman devoid of the usual lusts and frailties of mankind, who upon reaching maturity would institute a benign scientific rule. But the apparently successful experiment has a flaw: it instills into the girl a hatred for all men, and a ruthless cruelty. Her supernatural scientific gifts enable her to master atomic power, and practically leads her to destroy the world. She breaks the will and strength of men, and elevates women to positions of wealth and power. She also discovers human synthesis, and by this means she is able to escape retribution when she is eventually overthrown. She is seen to collapse and die, a victim of consuming ketabolism, echoing the memorable finale of Rider Haggard's *She*. In actuality, it was only her synthetic image, and this paved the way for the *Golden Amazon Returns*, and further sequels

Fearn sold reprint rights in the first novel to the prestigious Canadian magazine, the Toronto *Star Weekly*. The magazine carried a special Comics Supplement, the centre section of which was a 'complete novel', published in newspaper format. Aimed at a general readership, the novels were written by the top popular novelists of the day, including John Dickson Carr, Ellery Queen, and P. G. Wodehouse. They sold hundreds of thousands of copies, and the novels were syndicated to several American newspapers in the Maine and New York areas. The Amazon novels enjoyed extraordinary popularity (especially with Canadian housewives), and ran for the next sixteen years following the appearance of the first novel in the March 3, 1945 issue, ending with Fearn's sudden death in September 1960, aged only fifty-two. His final two Amazon novels appeared posthumously.

During Fearn's lifetime, only the first six novels were published in British hardcover editions from the World's Work in England, after appearing in the *Star Weekly*. This was because the publishers discontinued their entire fiction line in 1954. However, the Amazon novels continued to appear in the *Star Weekly*, eventually notching up twenty-four titles.

Fearn had resold paperback rights to the Canadian publisher Harlequin Books, but after publishing only the first three titles, they stopped publishing SF and other genre fiction to concentrate on their famous Romances line.

Meanwhile, as early as 1949, Fearn had realized that the Amazon series had the potential to run indefinitely. This presented him with a problem, however. The 'origin story' of the Golden Amazon was conceived and actually set during the Second World War. Subsequent novels were written during the war and the immediate postwar period, and projected their stories only a few decades into the future.

He very astutely realized that to keep ahead of reality, he needed to move the Amazon *further* into the future—first into the outer solar system, and thence to the stars. So with the seventh novel, he introduced a new main character, Abna of Atlantis—someone as equally intelligent, and even stronger than herself. These dynamics provided him with an *interstellar* canvas, thus ensuring that the series would remain ahead of reality.

Fearn's strategy was a great success, and the Amazon novels retained their popularity, ending only with his tragically early death in 1960. By then he had written a further twenty Amazon novels, and made preliminary notes for his next (which would later be written by Fearn's biographer, Philip Harbottle).

Long after Fearn's death, his entire Amazon series

would eventually see print from the pioneering US small press Gryphon Books in limited paperback editions, and later by the Canadian Battered Silicon Dispatch Box small press in their hardcover Omnibus series.

This new Borgo Press paperback series will be the first trade edition of all twenty-one of these later novels by Fearn, beginning with the seventh novel in the original series. First published in 1949 as *Conquest of the Amazon*, I have edited it slightly as *World Beneath Ice* (The Golden Amazon Saga, Book One) so that it can be read and enjoyed by new readers who may be totally unfamiliar with what had gone before. Subsequent novels have also been slightly edited for modern readers.

The publishers hope that this new series may create many more "fans of the Amazon." Meanwhile, any reader interested in seeking out the earlier six Golden Amazon novels will find that they are readily available on the internet, and in numerous earlier paperback and hardcover editions.

* * * * * * *

To date, readers can enjoy the following new Borgo Press editions:

Book One: *World Beneath Ice*

In destroying the threat of an alien invasion, the Golden Amazon had inadvertently caused a decline in the sun's heat, encasing Earth in an ice sheet that threatens to eliminate humanity. The Amazon encounters Abna, a descendant of Atlantis, stronger and even more scientifically advanced than she, and the ruler of an Atlantean colony still surviving in a protected environment on Jupiter. She refuses his offer of marriage, but agrees to form an alliance in order to restore the sun and save the Earth. One thing that Abna has not told the Amazon is that all the females of his race have been wiped out by a bacilli infection....

Book Two: *Lord of Atlantis*

A gigantic ridge of land rises from the Atlantic floor, causing massive tidal waves on either side of the ocean. Even stranger, both England and America are then assailed by an invasion of prehistoric monsters! A gigantic domed city rests on the newly risen plateau, whilst out in space an alien spacecraft orbits the Earth. Such are the mysteries and challenges facing the Golden Amazon, self-appointed governess of Earth, as she struggles to unravel the maze of mystery that was the deadly legacy of Atlantis!

CHAPTER ONE
HONEYMOON IN SPACE

Westminster Abbey in the late twenty-first century—not the time-honoured edifice of grey stone and exquisite carvings beloved of history, but a bigger and even more lavish recreation. Around it people in tens of thousands, packing the streets and paths and parks, all straining for a glimpse of the pair who were to be married this day, the most extraordinary man and woman who had ever stepped into Earth history and directed its destiny by scientific power—Violet Ray Brant, The Golden Amazon, and Abna of Jupiter, descendant of Atlantis.

The breathtaking loveliness of' the woman was something which held those nearest to her in thrall. She looked her eternal twenty-five, graceful in her oyster-satin gown. The bridal veil somewhat masked the shimmering gold of her hair, but it left the beauty of her features untouched. The mouth was full and red, the chin rounded but strong, the eyes a deep violet—unfathomable. Here was the woman who had a scientist's gift of superhuman strength and scientific intelligence, a woman whose brain had more than once saved the Earth from disaster and even rekindled a dying sun.

Yet still there was one cleverer—and stronger: the nearly seven-foot giant at her side. The grey suit he was wearing seemed inappropriate. He needed the toga-like uniform of his race. He was as handsome as the woman was beautiful.

The wedding was over. It was a signal for a stirring among the people. Among them, toward the rear of the mighty church, a slender man with heliotrope-coloured eyes sat musing. He was half smiling, a smile of scorn as if he considered this ceremony the height of absurdity.

Neither the Amazon nor Abna noticed him as they went on their way to a limousine that took them to the main London airport, where in a special enclosure lay the giant gleaming space machine *Ultra*, owned by the Amazon.

Honeymoon among the stars. That was the plan. Out in the wastes of space, once they had cleared the space-traffic lines operated between Earth, the Moon, and Mars by the Dodd Space Line, they could find the peace and solitude that only the limitless void could give.

The *Ultra* took off in a blaze of exhaust tubes; then the fiery trail ceased as the atomic power plant took over. The man with heliotrope eyes was in the crowd, watching the speck vanish in the sky. He smiled, again with scorn. Sefner Quorne, ex-adviser of Abna and master scientist, had plans of his own to put in operation while the Amazon and Abna were away.

Unaware of the intrigue in the mind of their sworn enemy—whom they had not seen since he had made an unsuccessful attempt to destroy all females in the Earth race many months before—Abna and the Amazon looked out on to the slowly shrinking globe from which they had come. They had changed now into attire more appropriate for their voyaging—the Amazon into a tight black suit with a golden belt at the waist; Abna into the toga-like costume of his race.

Mightily muscled, head and shoulders taller than the girl be had wed, he stood with his hand on her shoulder looking out of the main port.

"King and queen of Earth, Vi," he murmured. "Just as I said we would be."

The Amazon did not answer. Her eyes glanced over the switchboard at the automatic controls, then back at the massive atomic power plant. Even at this moment her mind was on the scientific issues upon which life or death depended. Any flaw in the mechanism or driving power of the *Ultra* could bring destruction.

"Nothing on our minds," Abna added, smiling down on her in the quiet, patronizing way she still found irritating. "No need to exert our knowledge or strength to crush some foe. Just you and I and the stars, and the future."

"Yes," the Amazon murmured, and gazed outside.

The endless stars were flung into infinity like diamonds on velvet. They were depthless, fantastically glittering, immeasurable. The sun blazed with his flaming girdle of prominences and eerie, space-flung corona; the moon sailed majestically, basking in her master's light. Venus, Mars, Mercury—and more distant, the orbits of the giant outer planets and their scatterings of attendant moons. And beyond it all, like a great misty sluice pouring out of infinity, hung the Milky Way Galaxy, the swirling core from which Earth herself had been born in forgotten time.

Abna said: "You said something about going to the end of the System for the honeymoon, Vi. Think we've got enough power to do it?"

"Had I not thought that, I wouldn't have suggested it."

Abna frowned slightly. "What kind of an answer is that for your husband? I only asked a simple question. You don't have to bite my head off."

"Sorry, Abna." The Amazon gave a faint smile. "I hadn't quite realized—I'm inclined to get brusque when I'm thinking about something."

Withdrawing from the gentle grip Abna had on her shoulder, she settled at the control board and began the complicated task of plotting the course through space. Abna watched her for a while, then he looked puzzled.

"Taking a chance, aren't you?" he asked. "Pulling in so close to Jupiter, I mean? You know what kind of a gravitational pull he's got; if we drop into it we'll consume nearly all our power trying to get out."

"It won't be the first time we've pulled away from Jupiter," the Amazon smiled. "Besides, our honeymoon would hardly be complete if we didn't pass close to the planet from which you came, would it?"

"But that's all over and done with, Vi. My own race and land are finished. You know that."

"Because the protective dome was smashed and allowed the poisonous air of Jove to sweep in and asphyxiate all your fellows—with the one exception of Sefner Quorne? That doesn't mean that all the machines are not still useful, does it? Jove—the mighty city which dwelt under the dome, and of which you were king—could be revived, Abna. It would be a tremendous addition to the forces of science with which we intend in time to ring the Solar System."

"Yes, it's a good suggestion," he agreed, "but doesn't it turn our honeymoon into a working tour? I thought we were going to abandon all our scientific notions for awhile and behave like a natural man and woman?"

"We are not natural," the Amazon said. "You and I are akin to god and goddess, Abna. Giant and giantess, in strength and knowledge. We can never be ordinary people."

"Do you regret it?" he asked, his hand returning to her slender shoulder; and she shook her blonde head.

"Not now. I did once. I used to think I would like to be on a par with Ethel, my foster-niece; or Bee, my foster-sister. Just a woman, with perhaps children of my own. Then I realized how different life can be when there is all the universe before one—when there are still unexplored worlds to conquer and rule. I had a plan once—the conquest of the whole solar system and its control by Earth with me at the head. I still have that dream."

"With me to help you now?"

"Of course."

For a moment Abna met the girl's wide violet eyes. They were darkly unfathomable as usual, masked by their big curling lashes. Her beauty fascinated him. But her manner he could not understand. It was as though the ceremony in the Abbey had counted for nothing. She was still the quiet, coldly calculating woman with whom he had fought a battle of wits before chance had put all the aces in his hand and, rather than be beaten, she had agreed to marry him.

"We've a long way to go before we're anywhere near Jupiter," she said at length. "Might as well have a meal and then relax. You fix it up while I make sure our course is correct."

Abna nodded and left the control room, heading for the big storage compartment where the essences and restoratives were kept. The Amazon watched him go and a thin, cold smile curved her lips. She continued with her course-checking until Abna announced that the meal was ready. With a nod she rose and went to the dining area. Her walk was steady, and the fixtures remained in place. Though the *Ultra* was hurtling at terrific velocity through free space, the gravity-nulli-fiers in the floor kept the weight down to earth-normal.

"I don't quite understand your attitude, Vi," Abna said, as he handed over the compressed food concentrates.

"No? You have the chance to read my thoughts, even

as I can read your thoughts. There shouldn't be any mystery between us."

"Shouldn't be, but there is. As for your thoughts, they are completely sealed. You've learned the art of masking them."

The Amazon smiled inscrutably. "Sometimes it's necessary, Abna. Marriage does not mean being bought body and soul: there are some things I like to keep to myself. Don't forget there are quite a few scientific secrets I have which you have not—and vice versa."

"But surely the very purpose of our marriage was to pool those ideas?"

"Later, perhaps...." And the Amazon withdrew into her own mysterious personality and said no more.

Abna was a man in every sense of the word: the woman he had wed was a woman in form only. In all the time he had known her, though he fancied he had analyzed her nature and thoughts completely, he had failed—as all men had—in penetrating the armour with which she had surrounded herself. The Golden Amazon's body and mind were infinities apart.

"Do you suppose," Abna asked, "that Earth will be safe while we're away?"

"Why shouldn't it be?" The Amazon finished her meal and sat back to regard him.

"I'm thinking of Sefner Quorne. You remember he sent you a letter saying he'd do all manner of things. If he does act, we'll be up against it, Vi. His science is far ahead of yours and mine combined. And don't forget you can't trace him, either. Now he has altered his bodily energy content, you can't put an aura-compass on him."

The Amazon frowned in annoyance. The aura-compass, that infallible instrument of her own design, had the power of pointing to any given person if the aura—the electrical energy—of that person were known. Until Quorne had come into the scene the aura of every living thing had been changeless: he, however, had accomplished the miracle of altering his energy, and, the new aura number being unknown, he was virtually undetectable. It was not a happy thought for the Amazon. Sefner Quorne might be anywhere, waiting to implement his threat.

"All I can say is, Earthlings must take care of themselves for a change, Abna."

She became silent again, as though waiting for something. Abna rubbed a hand drowsily over his forehead.

"I feel uncommonly tired," he said, puzzled. "A thing I've never experienced before. Sure the air's all right in here?"

"Far as I know."

He got up unsteadily, rubbed his forehead again, then went to the air-conditioning apparatus. The gauges showed it was functioning perfectly. He looked at the Amazon again. She seemed undisturbed.

"Not affecting you," he said, frowning.

"No reason why it should, Abna. I intended it exclusively for you."

"Intended—what?"

"The gas in the store cupboard. Didn't you notice it

when you went to get the food?"

"That tart smell? I thought it was some kind of preserving chemical you'd put in— You mean it—"

"I mean it was lethal gas, released by the action of opening the door. That was why I told you to get the meal. Maybe 'lethal' is hardly the term for a man of your constitution, Abna. It won't kill you, as it would an ordinary man, but it will numb your body and certain areas of your brain. Chiefly those areas connected with the will."

Abna moved ponderously and sat down with a thump on the wall couch.

"What—what have you done?" he whispered. "You marry me and then kill me."

"I haven't done either." The Amazon rose, tall, majestic, in her black uniform. Her violet eyes were wide and gleaming. "All I have done, Abna, is paralyze every faculty by which you can shield your thoughts from me. Shortly you will be unable to move, but your thoughts will be bare for me to read. Every secret you have ever had will be there for me to take—and your will power being deadened, you will not be able to protect yourself."

"A she-devil," Abna muttered, staring at her. "That's what I have always suspected. Wait a minute! Did you say you didn't marry me?"

"That's right. We're not married. We never shall be."

"But, the ceremony. The archbishop—!"

"The ceremony was illegal. As for the archbishop, he was a synthetic image of himself, controlled entirely by my will."

"I don't—believe it." Abna got the words out with difficulty.

"No?" The Amazon turned to the switchboard and snapped on the short-wave radio that still gave contact with Earth. After a few moments of sorting out the stations, she tuned in to the midst of a news bulletin.

"...was the marriage of Miss Violet Ray Brant to Abna of Jupiter. It is tragic that the aftermath of the ceremony should be marred by the sudden collapse and death of Dr. Cranton, the Archbishop of Canterbury, but—"

"Satisfied?" the Amazon asked, switching off. "As we passed out into space here, beyond range, my will power over him naturally weakened, until finally it lost its efficiency altogether and the synthetic archbishop just collapsed and became clay. The deception will not be discovered. His body will be examined by his personal doctor, who has been hypnotized by me in such a way that he will not detect the switch and will pronounce the death as due to natural causes, without need for an autopsy. He will be buried with full church ceremony. I stayed at this switchboard as much as I could so the amplifier could carry my will over the gulf. I didn't want the archbishop—the synthetic one— to collapse too soon. It might have seemed—strange."

"And the reason for all this double-dealing?" Abna demanded, still fighting with all his giant strength to keep control over his slipping senses.

"I have told you why," the Amazon answered. "I

mean to learn every scientific secret you possess, Abna, and so add your knowledge to my own. I could never have done it without marrying you—or apparently marrying you. Only by marrying you could we be together as we are now, on this supposed honeymoon."

Abna smiled cynically. "It shouldn't have been difficult for a woman like you to have pulled this trick without the farce of a supposed marriage."

"True, but I preferred it this way. I want all the world to believe we are married. I rely a great deal on the mood of the people. They will trust me implicitly if they think I married you; if they knew I had thrown you overboard just to gain more power, they might turn against me. So, let them think our marriage is genuine. I can explain away your disappearance as a space accident. By the time you are found—if you are—my position will be unassailable."

"Disappearance?"

The Amazon came and seated herself close beside the wall couch where Abna still wrestled with paralysis. There was a triumphant gleam in her violet eyes.

"I'm leaving you on Io, Abna—one of the moons of your own world of Jupiter. The Cosmic Engineers of the Earth government were instructed by me many months ago to come to this moon—and also Ganymede—to adapt them into worlds suitable for colonisation. They could be used as bases from which to mine valuable minerals in the asteroid belt—and the other moons in the Jovian system. It is merely an extension of the same work already being conducted on Mars, so that the colonists there will no longer need to live under protective domes. Following out my own designs, the Engineers buried within each Moon's core a gravity generator that would enable those bodies to retain an atmosphere. Deep shafts have also been sunk, to release trapped gases. These were mephitic and poisonous, but vast quantities of special bacteria have been released, which will convert it into what will ultimately become a breathable mixture containing high levels of oxygen and nitrogen, and also water. Similarly, certain genetically-engineered vegetation has been introduced that will assist in the process. The cosmic Engineers completed their work some time ago, and have now left. However, the "conversion process" may take several years before the moons are fully fit for colonisation. At the present time, Io is still a desert island of a world, where a man of your super constitution can perhaps still live, but where you will remain until the Engineers return to check on progress, when you may be found if you are still alive. Once I have your secrets, Abna, you cease to be of interest to me."

Abna could not say any more. He sat motionless, his eyes fixed on her. His mind was alive, his body temporarily dead. With his will suspended, there was nothing he could do to block the mental probing of the woman who sat opposite him.

She worked methodically, making notes, exerting her extraordinary telepathic gifts to the full. An hour passed, perhaps two hours, then she was finished. Abna still sat like a stone image. She knew everything he had ever known, had a complete grasp of every scientific secret. Only his innate metaphysical powers were denied to her, as this gift could not be transferred or learned in so short a time.

Rising, she considered him; then with a sudden effort she heaved his massive form on to her shoulder and carried him to the empty compartment at the tail of the ship, which had been left empty. She laid Abna down on the floor and then spoke. He could hear and see her even though he could not respond.

"The next stop is Io, Abna," she said. "There we must part. You have still a lot to learn about women—and one woman in particular."

With that she went out and pushed over the heavy metal clamps. Returning to the control room, she studied again the notes she had made, then satisfied that they were indelibly impressed upon her brain, she set fire to them and turned to the control board.

The *Ultra* had just cleared the orbit of Mars, and was hurtling through the emptiness of space safely above the plane of the asteroid belt. In eight or nine hours at present speed, the field of mighty Jupiter would be reached, and that of his attendant moons. The Amazon studied the deeps ahead, Jupiter already looming like a tiny ball with flattened poles, his cloud-belts girdling him in dark bands.

Setting the radar alarm, she got up and went to the small chamber that served as her bedroom. She threw herself on the bunk, fully dressed as she was, and lay thinking.

She thought back on the time when she had wondered if she really loved Abna. For a period she had believed in this possibility: the woman in her had overpowered the scientist. But now, so unpredictable was her ruthless temperament, the scientist was in charge again. With the knowledge of Atlantean science added to her own, there was nothing she could not do. Besides, Abna was a man—a godlike man, perhaps, but still male, and deep in the nature of the Golden Amazon was a burning hatred of the opposite sex. Its reason lying buried in the scientific operation that had made her a scientific machine in the vestment of the most beautiful woman the world had ever known.

Presently she fell asleep, regardless of the man locked in the metal room. But he was recovering rapidly from the gas that had paralyzed him. When finally all its after-effects had gone, he struggled to his feet and looked about him in the dim light of the single roof globe. He knew better than to attempt anything with the metal walls, his only barrier against the searing cold of absolute space-zero; so he moved to the door and pushed at it with his giant muscles. Nothing happened: the massive clamps were proof against him.

Finally he decided to wait. There must come a time when the Amazon would release him, and when that happened, tigress though she was, when it came to physical strength, he was more than her equal. Since she had renounced all love and friendship, she must play the game the hard way. So Abna relaxed, smiling grimly, listening to the steady throb of power from the atomic plant. By alterations in its rhythm he would be able to tell when the *Ultra* was moving off course and action could be expected.

At the first sound of the alarm buzzer, the Amazon awoke and hurried to the control board. The *Ultra* was just coming into the huge gravitational field exerted by Jupiter, greatest of all the planets. The Amazon swung the ship round gently, playing tag with the gravity fields, until the nose was pointing directly to Io, one of Jupiter's largest moons.

CHAPTER TWO
PLAN FOR CONQUEST

As the *Ultra* moved swiftly toward it, Io changed visibly from a rough, craggy world into something more interesting. There were deep valleys, heavily cratered plains and hillsides clothed with fantastic vegetation. Unlike the parent body, Jupiter, Io now had breathable air, most of it centred up to a height of three-quarters of a mile in the vegetation-covered valleys.

Io was a weird, fantastic little world, bathed in the triple lights of Europa, Ganymede, and the distant sun, to which was added the sullen green of vast Jupiter occupying all the sky. And yet, it was a world on which an oxygen-breathing animal could now live, which was more than could be said of the ammoniated-hydrogen atmosphere of Jupiter.

Finally the instrument showed the shallow air level had been contacted. The Amazon closed a switch and the *Ultra* came to a gradual halt, hovering helicopter-style over a valley.

The Amazon hurried to the chamber in which Abna was sealed. Taking her protonic gun from her belt as a safeguard, she pushed away the clamps with her free hand and then stood back.

"Come out, Abna," she ordered—and waited.

The metal door opened slowly and Abna's gigantic figure appeared. He looked at the alert girl, and at the protonic gun in her hand. To try conclusions with that deadly weapon would be suicidal, so he walked slowly past her into the control room. She followed him, her weapon keeping him covered.

"Apparently the stories I have heard about you, Vi, are correct," he said quietly. "You haven't a spark of decent human feeling in your make-up. You're nothing but a...."

"I'm not interested, Abna," the Amazon broke in. "Open that floor trap and get the ladder dropped. We're fifty feet from the surface of Io, and that's where I'm leaving you. You won't die. There is enough edible vegetation on Io to last you the rest of your life—and water, too. Not a very glorious end for the once-proud ruler of Jove, but necessary."

Abna said no more. He moved forward to the floor trap and began to slide the bolts back—then abruptly his hands shot upward instead and simultaneously gripped the Amazon's gun wrist and her throat. A vicious twist flung the gun out of her grip, and the clutch on her throat slammed her against the curved wall.

"Since you want it this way, Vi, all right," Abna said.

The Amazon's hands clamped suddenly on Abna's wrist as he pinned her neck. She strained her muscles to the uttermost and, powerful though he was, he had to give way because of pain in his wrist and forearm.

He brought his other hand up, then snatched it back as the Amazon's teeth bit into it savagely.

The instant his grip left her she brought up her knee and struck him in the stomach. He doubled, gasping slightly, only to meet the more-than-human impact of her right fist as it slammed into his jaw. He staggered a few paces and half fell at the bench in front of the control board. When he straightened up again the Amazon had recovered her protonic gun.

With her foot she kicked away the bolts on the floor trap and then lifted it back on its hinges. The air of Io came drifting into the control room, heavy with the scent of genetically-engineered vegetation. She snapped a switch on the control panel and from the bottom of the *Ultra*, below the trap, a ladder extended itself into the depths.

"Get down," she ordered coldly.

Abna considered her, then he smiled faintly. She wondered why. Then, without another word, he stepped into the hole in the floor and began to descend. When he reached the lowest rung and dropped lightly in Io's third-normal gravity, she closed the switch that returned the ladder into position and rebolted the trap-door.

Her last vision of Abna as she retracted the suspensory-screws and switched in the atomic power was of him standing on a rocky ledge watching the machine's movement to the upper reaches. He became remote, and then was gone.

Just as the Amazon was preparing to settle at the

control board, she was suddenly flung to the metal floor and held there by a tremendous surge of acceleration with which even the gravity nullifiers could not cope. At the same moment she heard the change in rhythm in the power plant as its load was nearly quadrupled.

Weighted down with the force of countless tons, the Amazon clawed her way along the floor, straining every muscle in a frantic effort to reach the control board. She realized what had happened. Abna, when he had fallen by the switches, had altered the delayed-action power control. She knew what it meant if she did not reach it. The *Ultra* would hurtle into outer space at inconceivable speed until every scrap of atomic power was used up. The acceleration, constantly mounting, would so crush down on her heart and lungs that she would become unconscious, strong as she was, until the power plant was exhausted and constant velocity achieved.

She reached the bench below the control board and lay panting. Then she began to strain upward. Her fingertips came within three inches of the controls— then she could strain no more.

She collapsed senseless on the floor.

* * * * * * *

To the southwest of London stood a residence apart from its fellows. Its tenant, a tall, austere-looking man of uncertain age, was not the type to attract attention. Jeffrey Carshaw was considered to be a wealthy bachelor who had retired to this home with a single manservant to escape the rush and bustle of the busy city.

Jeffrey Carshaw, however, was Sefner Quorne. To this home he had retired when his grandiose scheme for destroying the female sex of the Earth race had been beaten by the dual activities of the Amazon and Abna. Here he had lived quietly, his features altered by disguise, his whereabouts unknown by his electrical trick of altering his aura.

On the day after the ceremony Quorne sat in his library, pondering. Presently he rang a bell and his servant entered. He was the only other survivor of the Atlantean race whom Quorne had brought to Earth with him.

"You rang, excellency?" he asked, still clinging to the designation Quorne had borne on Jupiter.

"Yes. I've verified a suspicion of mine, Nalgo, and I think you should know it. It was not the real Archbishop of Canterbury who married the Golden Amazon and his ex-highness yesterday. It was a synthetic image. This morning I viewed the archbishop as he lay in state after his sudden demise yesterday. I chose an opportune moment to remove a sample of his skin from the fingertip—and my analysis in the laboratory satisfies me that he was never a real human being.

"The Golden Amazon created that archbishop from the original and held him by her mind until she was too far away to do it any longer. Then he collapsed and 'died'."

"Might I ask, excellency, why she did this?"

Quorne smiled slightly. "I have never succeeded

in divining the intentions of the Golden Amazon, Nalgo—nor, for that matter, do I particularly want to. All we know is that her marriage is not legal, which will probably distress his ex-highness quite a lot if and when he learns of it. However, the interesting thing to us is that we now have a lever by which we can perhaps win popular favour. Suppose I stepped into the scene and brought this archbishop back to life? What would the people think of that?"

"Excellent idea, sir—but do you know where he is?"

"Yes. From the constitution of the synthetic image—which is exact in every detail with its original pattern—it was possible for me to mathematically determine the archbishop's aura number. After that, the compass showed me where he is. The Amazon has no longer a monopoly over an aura compass, Nalgo. The archbishop is still alive and being kept a prisoner in a lonely house in Cornwall. I assume that several of the Amazon's most trusted confidants are keeping watch over him."

"She has taken a risk doing that, excellency. If he should escape, her whole subterfuge will be exposed."

Quorne shrugged. "Obviously she had some reason for keeping him alive, because she knows the image must 'die' with her influence removed. Maybe she even planned as we are planning to restore him from apparent death and strengthen her hold on the imagination of the people. That is by the way: we are going to act while she is away. According to her public announcement, she will not return for two months. We can do much in that time."

Nalgo asked: "Am I to assume, excellency, that having failed to achieve dominance over the race by destroying the females, you now intend to turn this planet into a scientific workshop for the conquest of the Solar System—and later the Universe?"

Quorne nodded. "We come from a race who hold power above everything, Nalgo. We have knowledge beyond anything these Earth fools ever heard of. We can dominate this planet by the science we possess. Tonight we will rescue the archbishop."

"Yes, excellency. And then what? The synthetic body is guarded night and day, and will be until the funeral. How do you propose to—"

"We have weapons, Nalgo, which can reduce those guards to suspended animation, their faculties moving so slowly they will have no idea of what is going on around them, and no remembrance of anything when they recover. The body will still be there, but it will be the real one, sleeping, until I am ready to 'restore' it. Yes, indeed, I can imagine how these Earth fools will worship it. Anything a little beyond their imagination they call a miracle. They have no scientific intelligence whatever, Nalgo."

Nalgo nodded. Whatever Sefner Quorne said was law—with good reason. Quorne's knowledge of science bordered on the uncanny.

"We have much to do," Quorne said, rising. "You had better come down to the laboratory with me."

Thus began Quorne's plan. At nightfall he and

Nalgo, armed with queer weapons, drove to Cornwall, guided by the unerring aura-compass, which showed exactly where the missing archbishop was to be found.

The minions of the Amazon guarding the archbishop stood no chance against the sudden electrical onslaught that hit them. One minute they were aware of Quorne and Nalgo making entry into the lonely house; the next they were dead. The archbishop, unharmed, sat in the big main room of the house, gazing blankly at the two men who had wrought such havoc in a few seconds.

"We are friends, Dr. Cranton," Quorne said. "I much regret this violent intrusion, but it was necessary in order to effect your rescue."

"Murder is never necessary," the archbishop retorted.

"You have been the captive of the Golden Amazon. Were you aware of that?"

"Certainly. She informed me that I was in some danger and so transferred me here. Knowing Miss Brant as I do, I am sure her methods were justified."

"Many things have happened while you have been in captivity," Quorne murmured, realizing the archbishop had been duplicated without his knowledge. "I shall now escort you back to London."

The archbishop rose, frowning. "Who are you?"

"My name is Jeffrey Carshaw," Quorne lied. "Your abduction has been a source of worry to me, hence my decision to rescue you. That these guardian murderers have been killed in the process I regard as irrelevant."

"And I repeat that—"

"Quite," Quorne broke in. Then his right hand

suddenly came out of his pocket and fired a blunt-nosed instrument. The archbishop found himself enveloped in a pale blue powder, which gravitated toward and settled upon him in a curious fashion.

"Asleep?" Nalgo asked presently, as Dr. Cranton became motionless.

"Atomic dust has many uses, Nalgo," Quorne answered. "He will not revive until I wish it. When he does, he will not remember what has happened here. Now, bring him out to the car."

Nalgo moved forward, lifted the motionless body on to his shoulder, then followed Sefner Quorne outdoors. The hardest part of the job had been accomplished. To deal with the men who were guarding the synthetic body in the Abbey would be child's play. Ahead of him Sefner Quorne saw his master plan unfolding.

* * * * * * *

The Amazon gradually moved, the tips of her fingers rubbing along the cold metal floor. A gradual tide crept over her numbed limbs, the slow return of life after many hours of complete unconsciousness.

She sat up, frowned. Gradually she remembered. The sudden whirlwind acceleration, her inability to stop it, the force that had crushed her into insensibility. Her eyes strayed to the chronometer. It had stopped under the strain.

She got on her feet, swayed dizzily for a moment, then had control of herself. The normal light had expired and the emergency circuit had come into operation. The drone of the power plant had stopped. She went over to it, her face grim. Every trace of the copper blocks, whose atomic energy provided the driving force, had gone from between the massive jaws. As each block had been converted to energy, automatic mechanisms had inserted a fresh block into place, until all the fuel had been exhausted. Then, when all the blocks had been entirely converted into energy, the *Ultra* had achieved a constant velocity—yet it seemed motionless to the Amazon. As acceleration had decreased to zero she had recovered.

She hurried to the outlook port and contemplated the void. Puzzled, she looked even more intently upon all sides, above and below. Still unable to believe what she saw, she mounted to the conning tower on the vessel's roof and examined the abysmal depths of space through the instruments. Every reading brought home the staggering truth to her.

She was well outside the solar system! Acceleration unchecked, the *Ultra* had reached an incredible velocity before the fuel had been exhausted—only a fraction beneath the speed of light, the fastest speed possible within the normal universe.

She was lost! For the first time in her career she was abroad in space without the least conception of where she was.

The speed was still being maintained at a constant velocity because there was nothing to check it. She was flying blindly onward into the unknown.

"And no fuel," she finished, looking about her helplessly. "I'm sure Abna would be glad to know how completely his plot worked."

To admit defeat was not the Amazon's way. She took the situation in hand and first revived herself with a meal and essences: then she concentrated on the problem.

Spare copper blocks she had none. To use the rockets to slow down her acceleration was feasible, but they could not last very long. The atomic dust explosive they used was only sufficient for a normal round-the-System hop.

An hour of solid thinking still left her no wiser than at first. The problem seemed to be insurmountable. Yet if it were not solved, the *Ultra* would continue hurtling onward through free space until it came within range of some heavy body; then it would immediately be drawn to it. This thought decided the Amazon against using the rockets in a futile effort to check her speed. She might need them yet to resist the pull of some alien gravity field.

At last she got up from her chair and went to the window, looking again on the incomprehensible void. She had never been frightened of it before, as long as she was within measurable limits of home—but here, billions of miles from all she had ever known, she found herself battling a rising tide of terror.

A sudden movement in the *Ultra* made her look about her sharply. She was conscious of it by the pressure against her feet. The giant machine was turning slowly. Through the window she saw the endless stars changing position. Her speed had not decreased, but direction had certainly changed and she could see no reason for it. The only answer could be that she had fallen into the attraction of an as yet invisible body.

Hurrying over to the control board, she set the instruments in action. The super-radar beam she projected gave back an answer. Tens of millions of miles ahead of her was a small but immensely heavy planetoid, uncharted, unknown as far as she was concerned, and towards it the *Ultra* was hurtling. There could only be one result when she struck that body. Vessel and planetoid would fuse into one, welded by the inconceivable force of the concussion.

Instantly she gave power to the forward rockets. By blasting toward the body with every vestige of force, it was possible that she might slow down her terrific speed—but even at that she could see no possible way to escape being disintegrated when the crash came.

With the knowledge that she had done all she could she remained at the controls, staring intently into the jet of space. Certainly her near-light speed was rapidly slowing. Slower, and slower still. Then she glimpsed the cause of her troubles ahead. It was a small planetoid, perhaps the size of Ceres, but with a strong gravity due to dense material.

The *Ultra* struck the planetoid. Then all sense of strain was gone. There was no shock, no jarring. And yet the *Ultra* was motionless, its titanic speed gone. The whole business was at variance with science.

She looked outside. The sun was a mere pinpoint of

light, but the radiance of the Milky Way and distant nebulae was sufficient to show a perfectly level land-scape, which looked like sponge-rubber. No hills, no dales, no vegetation, no clouds. It suggested there was no air—that this was some lifeless planetoid that lay far beyond her own solar system, but had been torn away from some other stellar system perhaps thou-sands of years ago, and was now a wanderer in the gulfs of interstellar space, far beyond the ordinary ken of intelligent beings.

Slowly the Amazon moved, utterly baffled to find herself still alive. Switching on the external gauges, she read them carefully. Her guess was right: there was no air, and the temperature reading was below zero. No place to venture—yet if she did not—?

She had scrambled into a spacesuit, snapped the transparent helmet in position, and with her weapon-belt well loaded, tugged open the airlock.

Gravity pulled her down the moment she stepped outside. It dragged her flat on her face. She rose only at the cost of vast physical strain. The amazing ground dented at every step she took and then sprang back into place with the resiliency of rubber. With her knife she hacked a sample of it for examination and put it in her specimen-bag.

The place affected her brain in the most incredible fashion. Each thought she had seemed to echo, setting her head jangling unbearably. She thought of Earth and home, and immediately the conception was slammed back at her with such intensity it swamped every other idea in her mind. Since she could not exist without thinking, it meant that every notion that came into her brain was reflected back to its source until she felt she would go crazy. Dazed, her head ringing, she clawed her way back into the *Ultra* and slammed the door. The queer mental 'echo' effect ceased immediately.

Here was a mystery of immense proportions, even to so skilled a scientist as was the Amazon. She spent a few moments recovering her balance after she had clambered from the spacesuit; then, since the answer seemed to lie in the planetoid's peculiar constitution, she set to work on an analysis of the sample she had brought with her. It explained much, if not everything.

The specimen was tissue and mineral in about equal proportions, just as a human bone is hard on the exterior with marrow and pulp within. Incredible though the Amazon found the fact, there was no doubt that, in a dim kind of way, the planet was a living thing. One titanic nerve-centre, but of such a low order of intelligence it had not the power of thought, only the power of reflecting them if they came from an outside source.

"Which accounts for my own thoughts being flung back at me," the Amazon mused. "This tissue-mineral reflects thoughts as a mirror reflects light-waves. It is vastly resilient, which is why when the *Ultra* struck it at incredible speed it absorbed the impact."

Then she remembered something. Once, when she had been with Abna, they had been being flung into space by a force beam generated by Quorne. He had solved the problem by his knowledge of the fourth dimension, in which space itself could be foreshortened to zero. The Amazon, in her recent troubled state of mind, had forgotten that she had learned every secret Abna possessed.

Setting the computers to work to check her equations, she arrived at the answer by one of the most complicated feats of mathematics she had ever attempted. Four-dimensional geometry was something new to her. She no longer wondered why Abna had wanted to keep it a secret: it unlocked the door to a thousand mysteries of space and time.

Theoretically, she knew now how to bridge the inconceivable gulf of space between herself and the distant solar system using only the minimal amount of ordinary rocket fuel that remained. Once she had done that she could radio to Earth or Mars for more supplies of copper, and so reach home—but first there was the practical problem of converting her existing power-plant into a four-dimensional one. Then she would need just enough power to give a ten-second burst of furious energy. That energy must envelop the *Ultra* and isolate it for a few brief seconds from the space in which it stood. Immediately before that happened she would fire the ordinary rockets to build up as much speed as she could, headed in the direction of Earth. After that, four-dimensional science should cause space to move around the *Ultra* instead of the *Ultra* moving through it. It depended on how accurate were the equations.

The Amazon went to work methodically, dismantling the power plant. Twice sheer exhaustion made her give up and rest. It could have been hours, days, or weeks that she toiled: she had no idea. She only knew she must not make a single mistake in the complicated conversion she was attempting. And at last she had it done.

Fixing the mechanical side of the business did not solve the problem of fuel, however—so, as she had done once before in an emergency, she sacrificed everything made of copper to the matrix of the atomic furnace. Terminals, earthing-rods, wires, struts, light-fittings, switches—the whole lot was torn to pieces and finally moulded at high temperature into a moderate-sized copper cube. This she firmly fixed in the jaws of the power plant and then gave the intricate conversion, now linked with the control board, a final once-over. Everything was apparently in order.

She made a careful survey of the unfamiliar heavens and, as near as possible, charted the approximate position of the planetoid she was on, then with the aid of computers worked out the approximate position of the Earth. Using what remained of her ordinary rocket fuel, she aligned the *Ultra*'s nose in that direction, then expended all the remaining fuel to build up as much speed as possible. This done, she was ready.

She closed the switch that operated the atomic power plant and waited tensely. The plant hummed immediately, and the *Ultra* became enveloped in a lavender light that flashed outward from the centre to swallow it in purple haze. To the Amazon the moments that followed were sheer anguish. She felt as if every nerve were being burned out, as if she and the machine were turning tremendously fast spins yet, paradoxically, without moving.

Space itself swung and warped before the Amazon's vision, and it seemed as though the stars were hurtling straight towards her.

CHAPTER THREE
RESCUED!

Just as Sefner Quorne had anticipated, the task of exchanging the real archbishop for the synthetic image had not proved difficult. The sentries had been reduced to immobility; the archbishop had been dressed in his robes of state.... When the sentries recovered themselves, they merely imagined they must have dozed a little in the weary watches of the night. The archbishop was still there awaiting the funeral.

At the service the following morning Sefner Quorne was present, and he made no moves until it came to the actual moment for the archbishop to be placed in the mausoleum. Then he came forward, ignoring the command of a policeman not to break the ranks.

The pallbearers hesitated as Quorne spoke, his clear voice distinct above the murmuring of the mourners.

"My friends, you have no need to mourn," he said quietly, and bowed his head in apparent reverence. "You believe our great friend the archbishop is dead. In truth, to you, he is—but he can be restored. I do not pretend to be a miracle worker but a scientist from amongst you who has found the secret of defeating the greatest of all enemies—death."

A group of policemen began to move forward, but the officiating clergy waved them away. The Archbishop of York, who had conducted the ceremony thus far, gave Quorne a steady look.

"We appreciate your claim, sir," he said quietly, "but this is hardly the time to demonstrate it."

Quorne said: "It is the highest achievement of science—something even the great Golden Amazon herself has not yet done—nor Abna of Jupiter."

"Your duty, my friend, is to allow this ceremony to finish in the proper manner," said the Archbishop of York. "Whatever you may have scientifically achieved should be demonstrated through channels other than this."

"Friends!" Quorne looked about him. "Is it your wish that our beloved Dr. Cranton should be restored? Is not this the right and proper moment to overcome death?"

There was no doubt as to the response. It became a clamour. The Archbishop of York, outnumbered, gave a shrug.

"Very well, since it is the will of the people. What do you wish to do?"

"I merely ask that the coffin be opened."

It was lowered to the ground and the lid unfastened. Quorne moved forward, a hypodermic needle now in his hand. Since he had openly said this was a scientific effect there was no need for him to resort to subterfuge. He depressed the needle's contents into the archbishop's bared arm. Then a stunned silence descended on the watchers as the 'dead' archbishop stirred and slowly sat up.

Quorne underplayed his hand. He reluctantly gave his name as Jeffrey Carshaw and admitted he was a scientific recluse who had many discoveries to his credit that were ahead of anything the Golden Amazon or Abna had devised. Then he retired from the scene, knowing matters would shape themselves.

They did. He was invited to speak on radio and television, attend functions, and outline his death-destroying system. He travelled about the world, lecturing, outlining plans—and observing. In three weeks he had accomplished much. He knew what his next moves must be.

As usual it was Nalgo who became his listener in the house on London's outskirts.

"We have the people of this planet at our mercy, Nalgo," Quorne said. "In the absence of the Golden Amazon they listen entirely to my side and not to hers. During my tours I have outlined plans for apparent social betterment—the marshalling of the people into different classes: the turning of each man and woman to the job he or she can do best. I can conduct a gigantic social upheaval, all in the apparent interest of humanity, without anybody being the wiser until it is too late."

"Do I understand, excellency, that by fitting every person to that which he can do best you are making the first move to have every man and woman an efficient slave in your master plan?"

"Exactly so. I intend to turn Earth into a workshop for the weapons I need to set forth on a conquest of the Solar System and the Universe. Venus is dead; we need not trouble over that planet. Mars is Earth-controlled, but must be brought into my orbit. Mercury is beyond consideration. Jupiter, from which we came, we may revive. Then onwards to Uranus, Saturn, Neptune, Pluto. We shall have opposition, of course, from the Amazon and Abna, but we can smash it."

"We may also have opposition from the people, sir, when they realize just what kind of a plan you really have."

"I am prepared for it." Quorne gave a grim smile. "During my recent touring, Nalgo, I contacted all the great men who really matter in Earth's affairs. In all there are ten—each man having the finest brain an Earth being can have. The ten comprise a mathematician, an astronomer, a military strategist, and so on. Suppose I pooled all ten minds in one and set it up as a mechanical dictator of the people under my own control? The brain of each man, separated from his body, mechanically fed, within a machine. All his thoughts and those of his contemporaries flowing into a common brain, the amplified thoughts of which will dominate every living thing on this planet and make them virtually victims of hypnosis. That way I can be assured of everybody doing my bidding without question."

Nalgo did not often smile, but he did so now as he

saw the possibilities. Then Quorne added:

"All this will take time, of course. We need to win an immediate army of supporters over to our side who can carry out my orders and abduct the ten men I have singled out. Also, we must put a guard on the space-ways, so that the Amazon and his ex-highness upon return can be dealt with. If they ever set foot on Earth again, it will be as prisoners. If they try to make a getaway into space, they will be pursued and extermi-nated. I don't intend to allow them to beat me a second time."

Nalgo waited respectfully; then Quorne motioned his thin hand.

"That's all for the moment, Nalgo. I will summon you when I need you. I have much planning to do, so see that I am not disturbed."

* * * * * * *

When the *Ultra* had disappeared from the deep violet sky of Io, Abna turned slowly and walked down the sloping valley side. He knew with unpleasant certainty just how bad was his present predicament. He knew the effects of the engineered changes affecting the little world. He could eat and drink, certainly—albeit by using his metaphysical gift to transform the still-poisonous liquids and vegetation into edible form—and he should be warm as long as Io's internal warmth—being released as gases to be converted—lasted. He could go on living in this desert island of weird plants and invisible catalytic bacteria, but he would always be alone. Nobody could ever come from Jupiter now his race was destroyed, and the chance of an ordinary space-traveller venturing this far in the foreseeable future was most improbable.

As he remembered the speed-control alteration he had made on the *Ultra*, he wondered if it had caught the Amazon unawares. Then he sat down in the triple lights of Europa, Ganymede, and the bulk of Jupiter to try to sort the problem out.

His gaze settled on Jupiter. On that huge planet, beneath a broken dome, lay the full resources of the city he had left behind him on his voyage to Earth. A city untenanted except by the dead, yet containing every needful thing, even space machines. But between the machinery and Abna there loomed 260,000 miles of empty space.

A thought stirred in Abna's active mind. He looked about him. The leaves of some of the strange trees were brightly burnished. They acted as mirrors, twinkling in the changing light.

Jupiter was not entirely devoid of living beings. Some humans still lived in the mountain ranges, sealed inside a dome—criminals whom he had ousted from his race to everlasting confinement. They had naturally not been given space machines, nor the technological resources to build them. Even if they had, they certainly would not help him. But there were also the Jovians themselves—the happy, immensely powerful, brilliantly clever natives of the planet, yet cursed—or blessed—by having no ambition whatever. No scientific problem was too profound for them to solve, yet they preferred to wander through the weird crystalline jungles of their terrible planet making no use of their knowledge. Abna remembered one of them in particular—Relka, a cheerfully impudent being whose sagacity had nonetheless saved him and the Amazon from death. He would understand a signal if he saw it, and was clever enough to fly a space machine this far if he were not too lazy.

It was the only possible chance. To try and get a light-message through to Jove and hope one of the race would see and understand the Space-Morse flashing across the gulf. But the chances of such a scheme working were infinitesimal indeed. Almost hopeless. The Jovian cloud belts would interfere with communication unhappily, but through the breaks something might be glimpsed. That would lead the Jovian who saw it to go to the heights—a trifle against the gravity to his incredibly strong body—and then something might be done.

None too sanguine, Abna went into action. He gathered all the giant reflecting tree leaves he could and transported them to the crest of the low hills. Time and again he repeated his journey, finding it no task in the slight gravity. In the windless air, even at the top of the hills, he spread the leaves out in an ever-growing area until it was large enough to catch the eye as a tiny speck on Io if seen from Jupiter.

To achieve the effect of cutting the lights off and on so they reflected Morse style was for a time a headache for Abna. He solved it finally by painstakingly passing a thin creeper vine through each leaf, drawing each vine to a long plait when every leaf was threaded. By this means a gentle pull raised the leaves, stiff in texture, to an angle so that they no longer reflected towards Jupiter. Dropping them back in place, they resumed their former brightness.

Then he settled down and constantly flashed out the single message—"Send Space Machine Here," using the Space-Morse understood by all pilots of the space-ways, but not by the Jovians—*except one*, and that cheerful, impudent being knew everything by reason of having read Abna's mind long ago.

Throughout the forty-two-hour-long day of Io he flashed his message with intervals for food and rest. Through the night—again forty-two hours—he slept heavily—to resume his flashing at dawn. He fully realized that the chance of Relka seeing the message was utterly remote, but because there was simply nothing else he could do, he kept at it. He calculated that nearly five days had gone by before something happened.

The vision of a curving "S" of sparks high in the violet sky brought him to his feet one morning. He watched with burning eyes. The sparks grew brighter and formed into a tail—the exhaust from a space machine. He frowned as he watched it take shape out of remoteness. It was not a Jovian vessel, but apparently one of the big Earth machines used for express services. Out here, though, it was far off the normal course.

He signalled again to give his position and then watched the machine sweep down under an expert hand. It came speeding in from the opposite end of the valley and landed. Waving his arms excitedly, Abna ran down the slope to it. The airlock opened as he neared it, and he stood in amazement, watching as familiar figures emerged.

They were Chris Wilson, Ethel, his daughter, Barry Schofield, her husband, and a stranger who was evidently the pilot. To Abna it was incredible, and none too pleasant, to find himself facing the family with whom the Amazon was connected.

"You!" Chris Wilson exclaimed blankly. "We saw the distress signal on our way past. Great heavens, Abna, what are you doing here? Where's Vi?"

"I neither know nor care," Abna retorted. "She ditched me here and then set off into space—I don't know where."

"Ditched you?" Ethel Schofield, formerly Wilson, sounded incredulous. "But Abna, you'd only just been married!"

"The ceremony was illegal, or so she said."

For a moment there was silence, then the grey-haired Chris Wilson motioned inside the vessel.

"Come inside, Abna, and have a meal."

Abna stepped into the control room and, while a meal was prepared for him he shaved and changed into a loose-fitting space suit; then while he ate and drank he told his side of the story. During it Chris Wilson exchanged grim glances with his daughter and her husband.

"Sounds as though Aunt Vi has reverted to type," Ethel sighed. "And I did so think she meant it when she said she loved you, Abna."

"She doesn't know the meaning of it," Abna retorted. "But I haven't finished with her yet, don't you worry! Once let me get to Jupiter and sort myself out a little and I'll give her a run for her money—if she ever comes back."

"Any reason why she shouldn't?" Chris Wilson asked.

Abna shrugged as he thought of the speed control he had changed. "I suppose she will," he said.

"She'd better!" Ethel said in anxiety. "We came into space in a hurry to look for her—and you."

"There are queer things happening on Earth, Abna," Barry Schofield said, and with help from the others he explained the rise of Jeffrey Carshaw to power.

Chris Wilson said: "That man isn't Jeffrey Carshaw. He's Sefner Quorne. I'd remember those unusual heliotrope coloured eyes of his anywhere."

"Quorne, eh?" Abna sat musing. "It's no surprise, of course. I knew he was around somewhere; so did Vi. As to his restoring the archbishop from death, that was simple, of course. Vi told me she had used a synthetic image. Evidently Quorne found it out and found the real man."

"And you don't know where Aunt Vi is?" Ethel asked in dismay.

"I know you love her a lot, Ethel," Abna responded,

"and for that reason I'd tell you if I knew her where-abouts. But I don't. She may be—anywhere."

"And unaware of what is going on," Chris Wilson said, frowning. "In that case, Abna, you'd better come back with us and see what you can do before Quorne gets too firm a hold. Vi will probably return in due course of her own accord. We'll waste time trying to find her."

Abna reflected for a while, then he shook his head. "Sorry. Chris, I'm not going back. I only ask to be left on Jupiter, in a spacesuit—with plenty of spare oxygen—and nothing more."

"But Quorne!" Chris Wilson protested. "Don't you realize that if he gets full control it means—"

"I am no longer interested in what happens on Earth," Abna interrupted. "Not after the way Vi has treated me. All I want is to be left on Jupiter, and then I'll sort out my own affairs. Maybe it won't matter so much if Quorne gains control of Earth. I don't think he can prove any more treacherous than Vi herself."

"You don't really mean that, Abna," Ethel said.

"I do. Either you must find Vi yourselves and get her assistance, or return to Earth and tackle Quorne as best you can. In any event, count me out."

And although Chris Wilson, Ethel, and Barry argued for half an hour nothing would change Abna's decision.

The distance to Jupiter being little different than from Earth to Moon, it was rapidly covered, and the pilot began to descend carefully toward the maelstrom of ammoniated hydrogen that formed the atmosphere.

"I'll take over from here," Abna said, motioning the pilot away. "I know the exact spot I want."

He settled at the switchboard and 'felt' his way down through blinding clouds to a point directly beneath the Great Red Spot, a continent upon which his city lay under its fissured dome.

A jolting quiver throughout the ship announced the end of the journey. Outside were low mountains forced down by vast gravity, writhing cloud belts sweeping over their summits. In the near foreground loomed the magical ammonium carbonate vegetation. To Abna it was commonplace, to the others a hellish fairyland.

"This is where we part," he said. "My destination is two miles to the west. If we ever meet again I hope it will be in happier circumstances."

He left the ship by the safety lock so none of the poison air of Jupiter could come within.

For a time the party stood round the main window watching him go, a bloated giant struggling against the screaming onslaught of the perpetual Jovian hurricane. Then at last the murky twilight that was the Jovian day swallowed him up.

"I don't like it," Barry Schofield said, shaking his head. "For he and Miss Brant to be at loggerheads is dangerous for everybody. They may become so busy trying to exterminate one another that Sefner Quorne will have a free hand."

"We'll get back to Earth as quickly as we can," Chris Wilson decided. "Our last hope is to hold the fort until Vi turns up—unless she's conducting some obscure experiment at the far ends of the universe. With her, you never can tell."

* * * * * * *

Two factors were involved in the four-dimensional experiment the Amazon attempted. One was the foreshortening of space, and the other—of which she had taken little thought—was time. It meant that in her transition from a remote spot in the universe she was not dealing in minutes but in weeks. A journey that normally would have taken years to cover—such was the relatively slow initial speed caused by her brief rocket burn—could not, even by foreshortening distance, be covered in so many minutes.... Accordingly, then, in what seemed to her to be anguishing seconds, as the stars themselves appeared to hurtle toward her, she made preparations to place herself into a deep sleep approximating suspended animation, fed intravenously by automatic instruments. Other instrumentation was set to deactivate the four-dimensional field, and then to awaken her as soon as she reached the inner solar system.

The journey that followed encompassed months of Earthly time.

Her first normal realization as the pain of the transition died away was of sunlight—yellow and golden— pouring on her through the outlook port. For just a second or two she did not dare to credit that she had accomplished her purpose.

She stole to the window and peered outside, slitting

her eyes against the unmasked glare of the sun. Her own sun! The inner solar system! She looked about her with a fast-beating heart. Only a few million miles behind her was the planet Mars, which meant that Earth itself was no more than 50,000,000 miles distant. The *Ultra* had converged into normal space again just beyond the orbit of Mars.

Almost singing to herself in relief, she settled at the control board and examined the apparatus in detail. It was apparently unharmed by the strange four-dimensional transition through infinite distance. She switched on the detectors to get her precise bearings. The next thing to do was have fuel brought out to her immediately. As it was, without any fuel, she would continue in space at her present modest velocity in space, but would inevitably be drawn very, very gently in the direction of the sun, his mighty gravity field gradually outweighing everything else.

The Amazon frowned. The matter of fuel went from her mind for a moment; instead, she was absorbed in the queer antics of the main detector directed toward Earth. The instrument was connected to the vessel's exterior and received all radio and other waves coming from Earth—but now it revealed waves which were not of the normal order. They were much shorter.

"Queer," the Amazon muttered, studying the needle-reading. "Can't be cosmic rays because the instrument is shielded; and it can't be gamma or beta radiation, or fourth-octave solar radiation—"

She stopped suddenly as she realized in what order

the radiation fell. Thought-waves! The ultra-short wavelengths generated electrically by a thinking brain—but thoughts of colossal power and range. Here was something she had never encountered before, and for them to be outflowing from Earth was even more amazing.

She thought first of Abna, then of Sefner Quorne, the only two living beings able to create thought on such an enormous scale. It could not be Abna—of that, she was convinced. In that case—

She snapped on the radio and immediately communications came through over the gulf. News bulletins, directives, orders to the people, propaganda on behalf of Sefner Quorne.... There was no longer any doubt of the situation. The Amazon got another shock when an announcer gave the date. Then she knew she had been absent from Earth over four months.

"Quorne," she breathed, clenching her yellow fingers. "So he has made use of my absence—and Abna's—to subject the people of Earth by amplified thought-waves."

No use calling to Earth for fuel: it would not be brought—yet fuel she had to have, not only to get her home, but for the even more urgent purpose of checking her slight but noticeable sunward drift. She tuned in to the space transmitters operating from Mars. The information she got satisfied her that as yet Quorne had not brought that planet under his control. She operated the private wave beam that gave her direct contact with the planet, and in a moment or two the face of Commander

Kerrigan appeared on the view plate. Kerrigan, with his wife, Ruth, controlled the Martian end of the Earth-Mars Space Line.

"Hello, Vi!" he exclaimed in surprise, recognizing her features on his own instrument. "Bit of a surprise! Where are you?"

"Some 50,000,000 miles from Earth and 3,000,000 miles from you. And stranded. I have no fuel. Can you have some flown out to me immediately?"

"Surely—but couldn't you get it from Earth?"

"I would, if Sefner Quorne were not running things. How much do you know of his activities? I've been away in space for over four months."

"I've heard all sorts of rumours," Kerrigan responded. "In the main, though, we get censored reports—not being close enough to view things at first hand."

"Quorne is in control," the Amazon said grimly. "And I've got to act fast to deal with him. Send that fuel on immediately. I'm drifting sunward. I'll leave a signal transmitter on so your vessel can easily locate me."

"Good as done," Kerrigan responded, and switched off.

The Amazon snapped the switchboard button and resumed her study of Earth. Though the instruments showed there were mental waves surging through the gulf, she felt nothing in the radiation-proof control-room. She ascended to the conning tower and by degrees removed the layers of transparent proofing over the hemisphere, until at length whatever radiation there was in space could affect her directly. She felt two things simultaneously—the burning intensity of cosmic rays and a slow, insidious compulsion in her mind, giving her orders, commanding that she do certain things.

With an effort, before her brain became entirely submissive, she returned the protective layers into position and the dominating effect vanished. She knew now what she was up against—a terrific hypnotic power that, on Earth's surface, must be utterly unbreakable. The only thing to do was insulate herself against it, and to this end she devoted the hours which must elapse before fuel reached her from Mars.

CHAPTER FOUR
SURPRISE ATTACK

In the *Ultra*'s laboratory she set to work to construct a tight cap of insulating metal—metal so thin it was transparent, yet, as she knew, capable of withstanding any known radiation except cosmic rays. The metal would certainly deflect thought waves, no matter how strong, and leave her mistress of her own mind while pretending to be hypnotized. The essential thing was to make the insulating cap so that it was not obvious— so on its outer surface she added synthetic skin and then synthetic hair, exactly duplicating her own in colour and coiffure. By the time she had the cap in position on her head, her own hair imprisoned beneath it, it was impossible to see the very thin line where the protective wig met the amber skin of her forehead

There was nothing more she could do now except wait. She killed a little more time by having a meal and a rest, then she checked over the deadly instruments in her belt to be sure they were all in working order.

Then a single refuelling rocket machine came hurtling out of the deeps of space, carrying supplies of copper blocks for the power plant. She transferred them through the safety lock, thanked the pilot, and then fixed a block in the power plant jaws. Since the plant was still in its four-dimensional set-up, she diverted the current to the rockets. When enough atomic dust had been exploded in the chambers to provide fuel—the dust being assembled much as carbon deposit forms in a gasoline engine—she began to set the *Ultra* moving, keeping a keen watch for any signs of her progress toward Earth being intercepted.

She noticed that the spaceways were unusually quiet. Normally there was a constant flow of freight and passenger traffic between Earth and Mars. The only conclusion she could arrive at was that Sefner Quorne had stopped the line working for the time being. What she did not know was that he had done so in order to know immediately if any vessel approached Earth—since he was expecting the return of the Amazon or Abna, or both. She also did not know that presently her vessel crossed the ray barrier that ringed Earth, causing alarms to be sounded at Quorne's headquarters and those of the guardian space fliers he had in readiness to ward off any attack. Their pilots, dominated by mind force, set off instantly into space to seek the ship that had raised the alarm.

The Amazon saw half a dozen swift fliers rising from Earth to meet her. She gave a grim smile to herself, and moved over to the protonic gun with which she had defended herself on more than one occasion. This apparatus could decimate any known metal, reducing it to its original atomic state. She also closed a switch, which by a current passing through the *Ultra*, polarized the light waves being given from it. It became invisible.

But invisibility, whilst a help, was by no means an insurance against attack, as the Amazon well knew. The instruments of the attackers would show where the mass of the *Ultra* lay, and they could release an onslaught against it.

The Amazon waited, one yellow finger resting lightly on the proton gun's release button. Being unable to control the *Ultra* as well as fight, she had set the machine on a level course toward Earth and was prepared to take her chance. She reached out and cut off the rockets. The flare of the exhausts could not be made invisible, so they had to be cut out.

Then the first three attacking machines came within measurable distance of her gun-sights. Her violet eyes fixedly watched the hair-cross until the nearest machine, already emitting destructive lavender beams, became exactly centred. Then the button was depressed under her finger.

The terrifying weapon had an instant victim. Space shimmered with blinding light for a moment as the onrushing flier was struck by sheer disintegration. It flew apart, its boiling core converting rapidly to pure energy. Five vessels remained and they came on steadily, their pilots blindly obedient.

Then under the impact of a deep orange ray from one of the machines she heard a plate crack in the rear of the *Ultra*. Instantly she swung the gun around and blasted the offender out of existence.

In normal circumstances the pilots of the four remaining fliers would have given up the struggle—but hypnosis kept them at their task, and the Amazon found herself grappling with new beams and vibrations such as she had never encountered before—evidently devised by Sefner Quorne.

She remained beside her proton gun, jolted at times as shattering energies ripped plates from the Invisible *Ultra* like slates from a roof. Another vessel she caught amidships with the beam and the two halves coalesced into devouring fire. Still three attackers remained as she continued her drop toward Earth.

Deserting her gun, she went to the switchboard and gave the rockets sudden power. Then she slewed the *Ultra* around in a circle and came up, invisible except for exhaust, under the nearest flier. She rammed it with terrible force, feeling the shock of the impact reverberate through the *Ultra*. As she sailed on, she looked behind to glimpse a dented ruin of a machine drifting aimlessly in the void.

Then the two remaining vessels closed in on her, using every weapon they had. The *Ultra* clanked and quivered as it ran a gauntlet of crossfire from various types of beams. Then suddenly the Amazon checked her speed with the rockets and swung around in a violent semi-circle.

A machine on each side was hit. One was smashed to pieces by the blow it received from the *Ultra*'s nose and the other was sent spinning away in a giddy top-like spin by the impact of the tail. Within seconds the Amazon swept the huge vessel back into position and got first one, then the other machine in the gun sight. They disappeared—and space was empty.

She smiled to herself. All six machines had been vanquished and the *Ultra* was still spaceworthy. How much damage had been done didn't concern her: she could assess that later. Right now her task was to reach Earth—and Sefner Quorne.

She checked her course again and then went to the locker-room for a suit of overalls. These she slipped over her conspicuous black tights. A cap effectively hid her wig of golden hair. Thus attired, she felt she had a reasonable chance of mixing with the public and discovering what was happening before she decided on a plan of attack.

With the *Ultra* still invisible, she brought it down gently on the coast of Cornwall. Here she had one of several secret hangars for her *Ultra*.

It was night when the great machine settled at last after its colossal journey through space. The Amazon switched off the power and opened the airlock, stepping out into the soft warmth of the summer dusk. She quickly found the concealed switch that, upon being moved, opened up a massive part of the face of the Cornish cliffs fronting her. She drove the *Ultra* into the gap, then stepping outside again, she closed the switch which returned the cliff face to its apparent solidity.

She knew Quorne had her aura number, and with a compass trained on her, her whereabouts would never be unknown. In this situation her only hope—and a slim one—was that Quorne was not aware it had been she who had been returning to Earth.

Moving along a narrow tunnel, she entered an enormous natural cave that lighted up with cold-light globes as she crossed a photo-electric beam. Here she set to work with the aura compass setting it to the respective aura numbers of Chris Wilson, Ethel, and her husband, Barry. In fifteen minutes she knew the position of each one. They were in a group in the heart of London, probably as mentally chained as the remainder of the population. This done, she tried Abna's aura number too, and had to wait for the needle to finish swinging before she could calculate his distance away from her. It ran into 400,000,000 miles, so presumably he was still on Io.

So Abna would not be likely to interfere with her plans. That was all she wanted to know. Her battle with Sefner Quorne was one that she knew would be deadly, but if she triumphed, she wanted the glory for herself alone. Such was the extent of her colossal scientific vanity.

Her next task was to make three more protective helmet-wigs, designed for Chris Wilson, Ethel, and Barry Schofield. These she stored away carefully in a pocket of her suit beneath the overalls. Then, a glance at the clock telling her it was not far from dawn, she departed from her secret retreat through a small trap-door, sealed it, and went silently into the starlit night.

A journey of two miles brought her to the main

motor road from Cornwall to London. She went along it slowly, an untidy figure in her overalls, until presently an old car came speeding up in her rear. She stopped and signalled with her hand. But the driver kept on going steadily. As it came on she took a flying leap and seized the projecting knob of the car's television aerial with both hands, whipping her feet from the ground at the same instant.

Something evidently stirred in the brain of the driver at this extraordinary feat of strength. He watched dazedly, at the same time glancing at the road to be sure where he was driving, as the Amazon crawled up on the car's roof. With hammer blows of her fist she smashed a hole through the roof until there was a fair-sized opening immediately above the driver.

"Stop this car!" she commanded, lying flat and peering down at him in the dawning light.

He took no notice—probably not so much because he was unwilling as on account of the hypnosis ruling his brain. The Amazon then reached down with her right arm and closed her yellow fingers about the driver's throat. With her free hand she kept control of the steering wheel.

The driver struggled savagely. The car rocked and swayed. The Amazon kept herself at a steady tension, guiding the car and tightening her fingers on the man's throat.

As he died his foot fell from the accelerator and the car came to a halt. The Amazon jumped to the ground, dragged the dead driver from his seat and pitched him onto the bank bordering the road. In another moment she was at the steering wheel, driving the ancient model as fast as it could travel in the direction of London.

It was around nine in the morning when she reached the outskirts. Deserting the car, she headed for the nearest pedestrian level, and lounging at a corner, watched the men and women passing. They were walking with curiously wooden movements, like manikins jerked by strings. Not one of them, as far as the Amazon could see, was in possession of his or her own personality—so finally she joined the throngs herself, moving like them deliberately, her eyes staring fixedly in front of her.

She then went to the underground and travelled to the station nearest the point where she knew Chris Wilson, Ethel, and Barry would be. Two guards at the exit to the station were checking identity cards as well as travelling tickets. Presumably everybody had a fixed purpose and destination—except herself.

When she reached the barrier she tried to slide around a particularly large man, but one of the guards shot out his hand and gripped her arm.

"Identity card!" he commanded, and studied her with a faraway look in his eyes.

The Amazon's right fist lashed up into the guard's face. He dropped unconscious, and in the commotion she made her escape and came to a huge factory, across the front of which were the words "Atomic Weapons Corporation." In two files moving in orderly fashion towards the doors were overalled workers like herself.

In this building, according to her pinpointing on the map after studying the aura-compass, should be Chris Wilson, Ethel, and Barry. So she joined the workers.

The sight of more guards ahead checking identities made her glance quickly about her. She went quickly to the side of the building, unnoticed by the guards intent on their checking. She came to a down-pipe stretching from the high roof, climbed it swiftly and gained the roof without mishap. Moving over its flat surface, she came to a skylight, protected by steel bars and with the glass frosted to prevent view below.

With one of her belt instruments she sawed apart the bars in a matter of seconds. With another instrument she silently cut out half of the glass, removing it with a suction cup. Then she peered below. A fascinating sight spread out beneath her. It was some kind of huge engineering shop, fitted with all the latest scientific devices, wherein oval shapes were in all stages of construction, and she saw they were spaceships. Hundreds of them, with hundreds of workers busy on their construction.

Taking out a tiny aura-compass from the belt beneath her overalls, she studied it intently, noting exactly in which direction the needle pointed as it came to rest. That satisfied her. Three workers in a group in the middle distance, unrecognizable in their overalls and caps, were evidently those she sought. She returned the compass to her belt and then considered how best she might get below without attracting undue attention. For at intervals there were armed guards. A mobile crane nearby was carrying an enormous bucket from which at intervals it tipped metal filings into a corner. The Amazon weighed up the situation and then nodded to herself. She was reasonably sure that the brief movement of her body into the bucket would not be noticed, and the next time the bucket was at its nearest point to her she sprang with all her power through the hole and landed in the bottom of the bucket. It was lowered to scoop up a mass of metal filings for transportation to the other end of the workshop. She scrambled out, burying herself quickly in the filings, and avoiding the massive bucket rim as it scooped toward her.

Emerging from the filings, she walked across the workshop, holding a piece of metal she had picked up to look like a worker on the job. So she reached and joined the trio of her friends who were assembling the shell of a space machine.

"Chris! Ethel! Barry!" she whispered urgently.

They looked at her without recognition and she found it a shock to see the vacant stare in their eyes. That the three were Chris, Ethel, and Barry, there was no doubt, but they might have been strangers for all the notice they took. They went on again with their work.

The Amazon glanced outside the shell. Nobody was nearby and the guards were some distance away. So she moved in again to face Chris.

"Sorry, Chris," she said quietly, "but I've no choice—"

And she brought up a left hook to his jaw that dropped him on his back, knocked out. Ethel and Barry looked at him in wonder, then at the Amazon.

Then they resumed their work as though nothing had happened.

Dropping to her knees, the Amazon pulled out the protective wig she had made for Chris and slipped it quickly over his head. It was impossible to detect that it was there when in position. Then she set to work to revive him. The look in his blue eyes as he began to come round showed that hypnotic control was no longer having an effect.

"Vi!" he whispered in amazement, staring at her as she held his shoulders. "My jaw! What hit it?"

"My fist," the Amazon answered. "Sorry. I had to fix a helmet on you so you'd be insulated against hypnosis."

Chris struggled to his feet, frowning.

"Where did you spring from?" he asked.

"Space—and I've no time to waste, Chris. What exactly is the position? Is it mass hypnosis?"

"Twenty-four hours a day," he answered grimly. "The whole world is under it. I remember returning to Earth after looking for you—and finding Abna instead—then I must have succumbed, along with Ethel and Barry Schofield and our pilot. I don't remember anything more until just now when I found you looking at me."

"Abna?" the Amazon repeated, her violet eyes intent.

"Yes. Why did you ditch him? We found him making signals from Io and we rescued him. We asked him to come and try and defeat Quorne but all he wanted was to go to Jupiter—so we let him."

"You mean," the Amazon breathed, "you left him to

perhaps resurrect that Jovian city of his?"

"That was his idea, I believe."

"Chris, you idiot! Don't you realize that he'll now do everything he can to hit back at me? As if I haven't enough on my hands trying to defeat Quorne!"

"But it's beyond all reason, Vi," Chris protested. "Why did you have to ditch him as you did?"

Her eyes flamed. "That's my business—and you'd no right to interfere. That helmet comfortable?"

"Yes—feels like a skin." Chris looked at Ethel and Barry. "It certainly makes people look blank, this hypnosis," he muttered.

"I have protection for them, too," the Amazon said—then Chris gasped as with unerring force and precision, she knocked out Barry and then Ethel, laying them gently on the floor. To fit them out with their respective wigs did not take long; then they began to slowly recover. Their bewilderment was as complete as Chris' had been.

"Now listen carefully," the Amazon murmured, after she had glanced about her outside. "As long as you wear these wig helmets you cannot be ruled by hypnosis—but you have got to continue as though you are. You will have the chance to see what is really going on around you, and wherever you can, you must sabotage Quorne's efforts. No blame will attach to you because nobody will know you are not under hypnosis like everybody else."

"We'll do all we can," Chris promised. "In fact, we've got to: you just don't realize how far this thing has gone, Vi."

"I haven't had time to find out," she responded. "Where does all this mental force come from?"

"As far as we know, Aunt Vi." Ethel responded, "Quorne had the ten cleverest men in the world abducted and their brains transferred to a gigantic amplifying machine in the city centre. Their ideas and Quorne's are all in one common pool, with him at the head controlling things. People are hypnotized and made clever at the same time. They build space machines and complicated scientific instruments without having been taught, receiving their knowledge directly from one or other of the enslaved brains."

"The whole world's become a scientific workshop," Barry Schofield said bitterly. "Quorne's idea seems to be to conquer every planet in the System; then set out to master the universe."

The Amazon said: "My next move will be to get to this brain machine and destroy it. Once that is done and the hypnosis removed, the people can assert themselves, under my leadership. You three know what to do."

They nodded and she glided from their midst, dropping into an automaton-like walk. For a little while she moved about the workshop as if engaged on special errands, then the moment the chance presented itself she took the place of one of the workers driving a truck to the outdoors—by the simple expedient of knocking the man out. Once in the big yard she faced again the same problem of getting past the guards waiting at the gateway. She drove the truck on steadily—then instead of slowing down as they blocked the path she accelerated to the limit. Regardless of the fact that she mowed down two of the screaming men under the heavy wheels, she hurtled the truck out into the street.

She jumped from the truck at a corner and sped swiftly on foot down a narrow passage between two big buildings, emerging no more than a quarter of a mile from what had once been Piccadilly Circus and the city centre. Slowing to a walk, she mingled with the throngs again, moving ever nearer to the heart of the metropolis.

The immediate problem was to find the exact location of the brain amplifier. The only likely clue she could think of was a transmitting aerial of giant size. She saw it finally—or at least judged it to be what she was seeking—atop a square building where Ludgate Hill had once stood. She made her way toward it and saw a veritable army of guards surrounding the place, they themselves being behind nine-foot high iron railings. The protection afforded the place satisfied the Amazon that it was the nerve centre of the whole grim intrigue.

It was mealtime, and she followed a line of people into a big canteen and was provided with a free meal of doubtful quality.

As she ate and drank she mused upon the problem ahead of her, finally arriving at the conclusion that there was nothing for it but direct tactics. Even if she were apprehended in her onslaught on the brain machine, it would be wrecked in time for the people to come to her aid—so the gamble was worth trying.

She left the canteen with others and then made her way to the squat building very slowly, summing it up as she went. For considerable distance around it no traffic passed and no people moved. It was obvious that hypnosis commanded them to keep away. Reaching a point where 100 yards of deserted space separated her from the railings—and guards beyond—the Amazon removed one of her instruments from her belt. It was snub-nosed and gleamed like silver.

She began advancing deliberately, pressing the button on the weapon as she went. Ahead of her there was no noise or confusion, only a sudden wafting of disturbed air currents as, shattered by supersonic vibrations, the molecules in the iron railing fell apart and gave her a clear path. The guards beyond were also literally shivered into dusty heaps as she fanned the beam of the frightful instrument about her.

Thus, without trouble, she reached the enormous closed doors. They seemed to be made of copper-bronze. Whatever the metal, it misted over, bubbled, and then vanished in hot air as the supersonic beam struck it. The Amazon hurried through the gaping hole and into a wide hall brilliantly illuminated with cold light.

In this huge expanse of polished metal there did not appear to be any more men on duty. But the Amazon advanced with caution, her gun ready for instant use. Without mishap, however, she reached yet another enormously thick metal door—and blasted a hole through it.

Beyond lay the astounding scientific device she was seeking. It looked rather like a gigantic edition of an old-time ticker-tape machine—a huge transparent hemisphere perched on a massive pillar raised three feet from the shining floor. Within the hemisphere were scientific devices that baffled even the Amazon. She stood gazing at ten gleaming ovoids linked by multitudes of wires to slowly revolving drums. She realized that brains were encased in the ovoids, but what magical process of transformers and amplifiers was used after that she did not know.

The brain amplifier apparently functioned automatically. And no guards were in sight.

She raised her weapon to fire, then gave a gasp as a thin pencil of energy shot from somewhere above her and flung the gun out of her tingling hand. She swung around, her face grim. On a gallery that ran the length of the room, three guards now stood. She realized that they had evidently seen her enter and had been hiding.

"Get your hands up, worker!" snapped the man holding the gun, so the Amazon slowly obeyed. She remained where she was, waiting, and glancing toward her own weapon ten feet away.

The trio came down from the gallery, keeping her covered all the time. She noticed as they advanced that they were wearing helmets, evidently insulated, to protect them from the battering power of the amplifier at such close quarters.

"The Golden Amazon!" one of the men said, as he recognized her features beneath the working cap.

"How does she stand up to the amplifier without protection?" said the second man in wonder.

The man who had fired the gun said: "Miss Brant, you no longer have control. It has passed into the hands of Sefner Quorne."

"And you prefer to obey him instead of me?" the Amazon inquired.

"It isn't a question of that. He has the power at present: you have not. Our lives would be forfeit if we didn't obey."

The Amazon glanced at the men's helmets. "Do those insulate you against this machine?"

"Yes. How do you manage to keep control of your faculties so near the machine?"

"I don't," the Amazon lied, deliberately looking harassed. "I find it a tremendous physical strain."

CHAPTER FIVE
FROM MISTRESS TO SLAVE

Then she acted—with that phenomenal speed which always gave her the advantage. Her hands dropped from above her head and she catapulted herself forward. The nearest guard had no time to fire before his wrist was seized and twisted with such violence he spun around and staggered away helplessly. The second and third guards fired, but the Amazon ducked and grasped the nearest man around the legs in a flying tackle. He crashed on his back—but he didn't remain there. Moving at lightning speed, the Amazon swept him up and flung him with her more-than-human muscles straight at the third man, resulting in both falling and slithering along the polished floor

The first man jumped up and made a dive for his fallen gun. He saw the flying figure of the Amazon hurtling toward him. Her fist came up at the same time and struck him on the jaw. It broke under the force of the blow and he went crashing against one of the pillars and dropped senseless.

The Amazon whirled and knocked down the two remaining men just as they were getting up. Then she quickly dragged away their helmets. The effect was swift. In the immediate focus of the amplifier the thought waves were evidently unbearable. They writhed, shrieked, and then died.

Hurtling across to the man by the pillar the Amazon took his helmet too. Even in unconsciousness he moved uneasily and then relaxed. The Amazon went over to her gun, whipped it up, then focussed it on each man in turn. At the pressure on the button they simply disappeared, leaving grey ash.

The Amazon knew that if Sefner Quorne came upon her, he would wonder how she remained unaffected by the amplifier—and that would mean he would finally discover her neutralizing wig. Once that happened she was doomed, and so the addition of a helmet ought to fool him.

She worked fast. Strapping on one of the helmets, she threw the other two up on the gallery and then again levelled her gun at the amplifier. She pressed the button—but nothing happened. That hemisphere, which was apparently glass, was evidently something very much tougher. Going closer to it, she peered at the glazed surface. She did not attempt to touch it. If it were a hemisphere of pure energy it would instantly amputate her fingers.

"You are wasting your time, Miss Brant!"

The Amazon whirled and fired all in one movement at the sound of the voice, but not having time to aim her weapon, she decimated the guard on the right hand side of Sefner Quorne, while he remained untouched.

He was standing in the broken doorway, a guard still remaining on his left.

"Drop your gun, Miss Brant." Quorne's voice was coldly deliberate.

She had to obey or be destroyed. The weapon clattered on to the floor and the guard came over to pick it up. At the same time he zipped open the Amazon's overalls and unfastened the gold belt from about her waist.

"Good," Quorne said approvingly, as the overalls were refastened into place. "My greetings, Miss Brant—since you are unmarried."

She said nothing but her violet eyes glinted. Quorne was attired in an easy-fitting, one-piece suit, a belt at the waist from which hung his gun holster. On his head was an affair like a skullcap. The guard also was similarly protected—and the one who had been killed.

"You have caused quite a bit of trouble, Miss Brant," Quorne continued. "It was a little while before I realized you had reached Earth; then I had to find you with the aura-compass. You wasted your time with that brain amplifier, you know. It is foolproof. What became of the guards? And Abna?"

The Amazon did not answer. Quorne gave a shrug.

"I assume you destroyed the guards, as you did the man with me," he said. "But that does not explain his former highness whom you were supposed to marry— and did not. What has become of him?"

"I have nothing to say," the Amazon answered coldly. "As to Abna, he means less than nothing to me."

"I see. I observe you are wearing a protective helmet. I take it you obtained it from somebody in the city? Or made it yourself?"

"I made it myself," the Amazon answered curtly. "As I came in from space and noticed the power of your amplifier here, I rigged up a device to protect my brain, otherwise I could never have got this far."

Quorne smiled thinly. "I have always admired you, Miss Brant, both for your scientific skill and courage. It is such a pity to have to kill you, but you leave me no choice. There is not room in the Universe for you and me. However, before you die, there are many things I would like to learn from you—and I shall. I am willing to admit there are some things in your science of which I have only scant knowledge as yet."

"I assume you are suggesting torture, Quorne?"

"By no means. I am not a sadist, Miss Brant, nor am I crude. I shall learn all I need, but not by torture. Until that time I am going to imprison you. I need to determine how much I wish to know before dealing with you. I suppose," Quorne added, "you have realized that once you are without your helmet you are at the mercy of the amplifier, and my will?"

The Amazon said nothing.

"When we leave here and are out of the immediate range of the apparatus—which kills at such close quarters—your helmet will be removed, causing you to be instantly subjected. Now be so good as to start walking as I direct."

The Amazon obeyed, thankful for the prescience

that had led her to wear the helmet. Obviously, Quorne had been completely fooled by it—and he could not read her thoughts as long as his helmet was in position, since it formed a barrier, even as did her own helmet.

Once outside the building, however, he suddenly snatched the Amazon's helmet away. Though she felt no change in her mental state, she deliberately staggered and allowed a faraway look to come into her eyes. Quorne considered her for a moment and slapped her smartly across the face. She blinked and controlled her rage.

"Good," he murmured. "From here on, Miss Brant, you are no longer the mistress but the slave. Keep on walking, please. The jail is only a mile distant."

* * * * * * *

On faraway Jupiter, Abna was at the close of a protracted period of repair. With the assistance of the lazy but ingenious natural inhabitants of the planet, he had succeeded in rebuilding the breach in the great dome that covered his city. Then had come the task of starting the air pumps to work again and reconditioning the machinery. Now it was all accomplished. The one-time busy city was habitable again—warm and well-lighted—an outpost in the tumult of poisonous gases that comprised Jupiter's atmosphere.

One by one, as their work was finished—their reward being giant bottles of ammonia crystals for eating purposes—the Jovians had departed, leaving only one of their race behind—the one who had directed their operations and seemed to have a particular affinity for Abna.

Man and creature were together in the immense laboratory, its forty-acre area covered with complicated machinery and instruments. Abna, in the toga-like raiment of his race, was preoccupied, a fact which presently became noticeable to the Jovian watching him. He asked a question, using his normal method of telepathy.

"Something wrong, friend?"

"Everything's wrong," Abna growled back, and though he did not communicate by telepathy—the normal method of the Jovians—the thought behind his words reacted in the same way.

The Jovian was silent, evidently reading Abna's mind. He in turn looked worriedly at the fantastic creature who had helped him so loyally. The Jovian stood three feet tall and had the contour of man, otherwise he was not unlike a small ape in a coat of mail. His arms and legs were blocks, testifying to Jupiter's merciless gravity. His eyes were yellow but sagacious, his mouth fanged.

"You are going around in circles, friend," he pronounced, helping himself to a palm full of ammoniated crystals from a bottle on the bench and chewing them with relish. "One man alone here is no use. You need the woman. The Golden Amazon."

"That's right," Abna muttered. "I thought I had her, but she betrayed me. Learned all my secrets and then marooned me."

"So your mind tells me. You can't leave things that way. To have all this science around you and no race to perpetuate it is absurd. If you can't perpetuate it, why did you go to such effort to get things rebuilt?"

"Because I believed I could trace the Amazon in outer space and bring her back—but now I find the instruments don't react at all. I have had an aura-compass beam in operation to infinity, but she doesn't seem to be anywhere."

"That's your fault," the Jovian said frankly. "You shouldn't have altered that speed setting. Maybe you've hurled her beyond all signs of tracing."

Abna shrugged. Plainly, every detail of the things he had done was exposed for the weird creature to read. The Jovian cracked crystals in his fangs for a while and then said:

"Your aura-compass beam is fixed, is it not? Pointing in a certain direction? That is, it doesn't have free influence on all sides as a normal compass does?"

"Normally it behaves like an ordinary compass, but in the case of great distances a directional beam is needed.... I've examined space as far as possible beyond Pluto and there's no reaction."

"Have you examined Earth?"

"Why, no," Abna said. "But it's most unlikely Vi can be there. If she went into the outer deeps of space, she'd never get back for years—if at all."

"I think," the Jovian said, "that you greatly underestimate the intelligence of that woman. When I met her, she struck me as being exceptionally brilliant—even more so than you yourself. I should say it is possible she found a way back to Earth in spite of what you did to her. Anyway, turn your compass that way instead of towards the outer deeps."

Abna nodded. Switching on the current that actuated the sensitive needle with its diamond tip, he altered the directional beam so that it flashed to Earth at the speed of light. He waited an interval for the beam to make its trip, the Jovian watching the vacuum-cased instrument over his shoulder.

Tuned in the Amazon's aura-radiation, the needle suddenly quivered and swung, becoming steady after a moment or two. Abna's eyes widened and he promptly pressed the button of the distance reader. The needle swung up and down gently like a seesaw, and by carefully noting the number of swings before it came to rest, Abna was able to calculate distance and position.

Silent, his movements full of tensed excitement, he studied his detailed map of Earth.

"You were right!" he said at last, swinging round. "She is on Earth—at this point in central London. How she got there I don't know. Where do you get these bright ideas from, Jovian?"

"The lazy mind looks for the obvious answer," the Jovian replied, grinning. "Since she's there, all you have to do is bring her here."

"First I have to find out exactly what she is doing."

Abna crossed the great laboratory quickly, the Jovian waddling behind him, and switched on the powerful x-ray television beam. Penetrating all barriers once it had passed through a special slot in the impregnable dome over the city, the carrier wave stabbed outwards to Earth, invisible, but nonetheless a probing finger once it reached its destination.

Abna operated the complicated controls and numbered dials carefully, watching the giant screen upon which would presently appear the light-photons picked up by the beam and drawn back to the transformers in this Jovian laboratory.

After several minutes the screen glowed into life; as though viewed from an airplane at a thousand feet the sprawling mass of London became visible. Abna adjusted the focus and the beam passed through solids, thereby enabling him to see within the buildings.

The things he saw in his search for the exact spot where the Amazon was situated made his face become grim. There were endless arsenals stacked to the roofs with all manner of bombs; workshops operating at high pressure in the construction of weapons and space machines; laboratories loaded with scientific instruments.

"Things have gone further than I ever imagined," Abna said, his voice troubled. "It's obvious that those people there are working under hypnotic orders. Their expressions show it.... This array of power means that sooner or later I'll be attacked, and single-handed I can't defend myself, in spite of having a good defence. As for Earth, it doesn't look as though Vi has been able to do much."

"I thought you were looking for her," the Jovian

remarked.

"I was—until all this attracted my attention." Abna consulted the map again, rearranged the setting of the amazing instrument, and then watched the screen blur and dissolve into a change of scene.

It revealed a slender figure in shabby overalls sprawled on a bunk in a dimly lighted area. Beyond the figure was the shadow of bars on the wall. Abna studied the screen intently.

"Yes, it's Vi," he muttered. "In prison, apparently."

He switched off and stood thinking, his eyes meeting those of the hideous Jovian.

"It means," the creature said, "that for the sake of your own world here, and for the sake of the Amazon's planet, you must again combine forces to defeat Quorne—otherwise he'll destroy both of you."

Abna nodded, realizing his own thoughts on the matter had been accurately read.

"This gives me a lever," he said. "A logical reason for again bringing Vi to my side. Obviously, I dare not go to Earth and try to rescue her. Quorne would destroy me. So I must bring her here—by atomic disassembly."

The Jovian nodded. His queer, scientific mind knew exactly what was meant. A disintegrative beam would be projected to Earth to the spot where the Amazon was. It would dissolve her completely into her basic atomic make-up; then magnetic power would draw the 'parcel' of atoms back along the beam and reassemble them in this laboratory. It was radio-television involving organic fundamentals.

"Once I've done that and she is at my side once more, we can bury the past and try again," Abna said, his eyes gleaming.

With the aid of computers he began calculating the mathematical procedure necessary to project the dissembler beam across 400-million miles of space.

Unaware of being observed over the gulf of space, or of the plans of Abna concerning her, the Amazon lay for a while on the bunk in her prison cell. Her one advantage at the moment was that Quorne believed her to be in the grip of hypnosis.

Presently she got up and went over to the barred door. It was a solid piece of metal except for a small square at the top where inch-thick rods were welded in position. She examined them, decided there was not enough gripping room for her to attempt to break them, and then she stood listening. There were no sounds or voices or the feet of sentries. After a while it occurred to her that the prison was perhaps unguarded since hypnosis was in control, under which influence she, like everybody else who was not with Quorne's retinue, was supposed to be held.

She went to the window. It was no more than eighteen inches square and protected by three inch-thick bars. Outside was a stretch of yard with a high wall at its extremity. The yard was deserted, and from what little she could see of neighbouring parts of the prison, there did not seem to be any activity there either. Perhaps she was the only person in the prison, those who had been in it having become workers, held under control.

Leaping the short distance up to the ledge of the window, she squatted and seized hold of the bars, pulling on them gently to assess their resistance. Finally she decided on action. Interlacing her arms in and out of the bars and bracing her feet on the stonework within the cell, she threw every ounce of her muscular power into a sudden effort.

The bars crushed into the flesh of her forearms so that she winced with pain, but she did not relax her pressure. Her first effort brought the outermost bars slightly inward toward each other. She rested for a moment or two and then tried again, hurling all her power into the right-hand outer bar. Gradually the bar twisted, and finally it suddenly gave way from its support in the stonework and dropped the Amazon to the floor with the bar in her hand.

She used the bar as a lever against its neighbour, smashed it out of position, and then wriggled through the opening on to the outer ledge. She still retained the bar as her only weapon. To the ground it was about twenty feet. Slipping the bar in the pocket at the back of her overalls, she slid over the ledge, hung by her hands for a moment, and then dropped with her knees flexed to the stone below. She jarred herself, but otherwise was unhurt. Intently she looked about her. No signs of alarm; no guards. It seemed a certainty now that hypnosis was the only guardian.

She began moving slowly, crouched by the high wall, the bar of iron back in her hand. She little knew that her escape from the prison had caused profound bewilderment to Abna 400,000,000 miles away. His dissembler beam had struck the cell just as she had left it, with the result that he found his effort to abduct her in atomic form had failed.

The Amazon finally reached the massive gateway. It was barred on the exterior, so she climbed up it, using the projecting knobs of the massive hinges. Very carefully she finally peered over the top of the gate. Before her was a length of deserted street and, at the end of it, busily moving traffic.

Her objective was still the room where the machine brain was housed, but it would be suicide to attempt anything without instruments to protect herself. Her nearest laboratory was in the heart of the city and, granting Quorne and his minions had not discovered it, would amply serve her needs and give her a chance to rest and prepare for action. The one infuriating drawback was that Quorne could follow her movements with his aura compass, unless he were satisfied she was incapable of escape.

The risk had to be taken. She dropped over the gate's other side, and keeping her bar of iron concealed in her sleeve, she hurried to where the people were passing to and fro, and mingled with them.

Then, as she progressed, she began to notice that she had been in this region before quite recently. Yes, of course! Ahead of her was the very factory where Chris, Ethel, and Barry worked.

Then she saw them being led across the factory's huge yard by three guards. They vanished in a big brick extension and a door closed.

She reached the wall of the factory and followed its base until it took a sharp turn. Here the main road was out of sight and nobody was in view. The Amazon sprang to the top of the wall, and wriggling along, she came to within jumping distance of the low-roofed annex into which the guards and her three colleagues had gone. She dropped from the wall, hurtled across the intervening space of concrete, then slammed her iron bar down on the window of the building. The glass shattered to reveal that Chris, Ethel, and Barry were securely bound to upright posts supporting the roof. The guards had whips in their hands. They stood staring at the interruption. The Amazon jumped through the window and flung herself behind one of the pillars as the nearest guard fired at her. The metal of the pillar smoked.

Apparently Chris, Ethel, and Barry were still wearing their insulated caps, for they were watching the proceedings tensely, clearly wondering how the Amazon had happened so opportunely in their midst. She herself remained behind the pillar, sideways, listening to the footsteps of the guards as they came nearer and nearer to her, waiting to close in and fire.

It was one of those moments when she had to risk everything—and she did. Tensing herself, she leaped for the safety of the next pillar, but she was not quite quick enough. White-hot fire caught her across the right shoulder. The numbing shock of it made her senses swim and she crashed to the metal floor, her wits blacked out.

The guards, protection-helmets on their heads, looked at one another. One of them said: "Better not kill her: that's for Quorne to say. I'll tell him she's here."

He went over to a nearby visiphone and gave his news to headquarters, then he returned to the fallen Amazon and considered her.

"Fasten her to one of the pillars like the rest of 'em," he instructed, and stood watching while it was done.

Finally the Amazon was corded up tightly to the fourth pillar in the annex, but she was no longer unconscious. The movement of being tied up had revived her. Except for the numbness the ray had created in her shoulder muscles, she was very much herself—but she remained like one dead.

"Now to you three," the leading guard said, cracking his whip. "You have found a means of defeating the control of the hypnosis and we mean to know what it is. Further, you have sabotaged much of the work being done in the factory."

The lash whistled through the air and from Ethel there came a gasp of pain.

The rope broke about the Amazon's upper arms. Again the lash descended and Ethel screamed.

Barry Schofield shouted hoarsely: "Let her alone! I'll tell you—"

"Tell them nothing, any of you!" the Amazon snapped.

The guards swung round in amazement to look at

her. They had not even thought she was conscious, let alone breaking free. With a final mighty effort she snapped the cords that held her waist and ankles and hurtled forward. Her bar of iron was a distance away, but she still had her fists, and, regardless of the pain it gave her damaged shoulder she slammed her right fist into the face of the staring guard nearest her.

He more than fell over; he flew backward and dropped motionless, his teeth and nose crushed by the violence of the blow. Quickly the remaining guards had their guns out, but they never used them. Lashing out her left leg the Amazon kicked the feet from under the guard with the whip. The other one she seized by the arm, spun him round, then brought her left fist down on the back of his neck with such force the vertebrae clicked. His knees buckled and he dropped on his face, dead. The remaining man crouched, waiting. He crouched even lower as the Amazon snatched up the whip, her violet eyes aflame.

The lash descended, and the guard yelled as the vicious tail cut through his uniform and flayed his back. At the end of the onslaught, he lay gasping by the wall, his uniform cut to ribbons, blood streaking him from head to foot.

"Your friends have apparently already taken a journey into the unknown," the Amazon said coldly, flinging the whip away. "You may as well join them."

She went across to the iron bar and picked it up. Chris, Ethel, and Barry looked away as the bar descended. When they turned again the Amazon was cutting their ropes with a knife taken from one of the guards.

She caught Ethel by the shoulders and held her tightly as the girl swayed faintly for a moment.

"Two slashes and you totter, Ethel?" the Amazon asked drily. "Come on, now!"

"I'll—I'll be all right," Ethel muttered, recovering as Barry took hold of her. "But those cuts hurt!"

"So did my shoulder—" The Amazon glanced at it. "Anyway, why did you give yourselves away?"

"Just the way it happened," Barry said. "And we've got to be on the move. That guard phoned to Quorne while you were unconscious. He'll be here any moment."

The Amazon dived for a gun from the belt of the nearest guard, Chris Wilson hurrying to another guard.

Then the skylight above was shattered, and Quorne and three men—all of them helmeted—projected their guns downward.

"Stand straight, Miss Brant, and raise your hands," Quorne ordered. "And the rest of you! Quickly!"

Beaten, her mouth set in fury, the Amazon had to obey. She, Chris, Ethel, and Barry drew into a tight quartet as, one man remaining in the skylight to cover them, Quorne and the two other men descended the outside of the building to ground level. In a moment or two they came in. Quorne glanced at the three dead guards, then back to the Amazon's angry beauty.

"I have to admit, Miss Brant, that you are more than a handful," he said. "You escaped prison and have defeated hypnosis. I congratulate you. You might even have escaped me altogether had I not been warned from here. I was so sure you were safely put away I did not even trouble to keep track of you."

Quorne's expression changed. His thin face became stonily malignant. "You have a way of defeating hypnosis, Miss Brant, without need of a helmet. What is that way?"

The Amazon did not respond.

"I might believe," Quorne continued, "that you, Miss Brant, overcome hypnosis by sheer will power, knowing the strength of your mentality—but I cannot believe it of these friends of yours."

"When does the cat-and-mouse game finish, Quorne?" the Amazon demanded. "Why don't you act instead of talking so much?"

"I was just wondering how best to learn from you your anti-hypnosis method. I would like it for myself. It would be so much better than this clumsy helmet idea of mine. Trust a woman—and such a woman!—to think of refinement. I am afraid physical suffering would not make you talk, Miss Brant. I notice how calmly you are taking that bad gash on your shoulder, but possibly such methods might work on Mrs. Schofield."

"You told me you never indulged in such methods," the Amazon said.

"As a rule I abhor them, but after all, if one is to learn something, it is necessary to take it out of the flesh perhaps."

The Amazon snapped: "These three are merely pawns in the game: they do as I ask. It is I whom you

hate, Quorne; therefore, it is upon me you should prac-
tise any atrocity you may have in mind."

"But they know the secret as much as you, Miss
Brant, otherwise they would not be invulnerable—as
they are."

CHAPTER SIX
UNITED IN THE CAUSE

The Amazon waited no longer. The sands were running out. Unwittingly Quorne had drifted closer as he had talked, so absorbed in his subject his gun had more or less drooped a little from its original position. He realized his mistake when with savage speed the Amazon's right hand clamped on his gun wrist and forced it downward. Helpless in her grip, he was twirled about and then held tightly before her, her left arm imprisoning his waist so suffocatingly tight he could hardly breathe, his gun hand twisted backward until he dropped the weapon.

"Now," the Amazon murmured in his ear. "You're going to suffer yourself, Quorne! With you destroyed, this whole rotten empire of intrigue you've built up will collapse. I can soon deal with your guards once I've settled with you—and I'm going to right now."

Spurred with the imminence of death, Quorne suddenly stooped forward, the only move he could make. He felt the Amazon's strong, supple body pressing hard against his back as he dragged at her. His free left hand shot up and caught her around the back of the neck. Though not a man of large physique, Quorne was wiry from many years of existence in the iron gravity of Jupiter. It stood him in good stead now.

Lifted from her feet by the grip at the back of her neck, the Amazon could do little. She doubled over his back, then her head hit the stone floor with stunning force. Dazed for a moment she lay on her back—but only for a moment. Her hand shot out, gripped Quorne's ankle and flung him over. Then with a quick twist she was on top of him, one knee in his spine and her interlocked fingers dragging up beneath his chin.

He struggled savagely as he realized what was coming. Inevitably his back or neck would break under the strain as the Amazon increased it. Quorne, pinned down, his guards afraid to fire for fear of hitting him, found his head forced up further. Then a last desperate move made him bring his hands upward. They clutched the Amazon's hair and pulled savagely. Instead of her head coming down toward him, he discovered something was in his hands and the Amazon herself had collapsed.

He relaxed, puzzled, staring at his hands and the mass of golden hair and flexible metal forming its foundation. Then he understood. He heaved the Amazon away from him and got on his feet. She lay, breathing hard, her eyes glazed with the crushing force of hypnosis.

"Very clever," Quorne commented. "A wig and helmet all in one—which I assume is used in the case of you three as well."

He strode forward and whipped the wigs from Chris, Ethel, and Barry in turn. Immediately they became blank-faced and immovable. The guards looked at one another as Quorne stuffed the wigs in his pocket. Then he went over to the Amazon and hauled her to her feet. The slap he gave her across the face only made him stare at her all the more fixedly. She had no real idea what was happening. Her mind was swamped by a confusing turmoil of orders and directions, hypnotically being given off, none of which she could understand.

"Each person," Quorne told her deliberately, "has a fixed beam in the hypnotic order and obeys the orders of that beam. At the moment your three friends are off key and must be put back, when they will resume work with blind obedience as before. As for you, Miss Brant, I'd be a fool to have you as a worker. I'm going to kill you."

The Amazon stared back at him. His words were plain enough to her, and they made grim sense, but she was powerless to say anything or make a single movement to protect herself.

"You are a believer in total destruction, Miss Brant," Quorne continued. "So am I. Leave no trace but the atomic dust. Unfortunately I have no weapon with me that can produce that effect, but I know of something equally useful. Please start moving."

The Amazon obeyed, leaving the annex under directions without so much as a second glance at the motionless Ethel, Chris, and Barry. She walked deliberately across the yard to another low building adjoining the factory. Here, as Quorne came up behind her and barked a command, she halted. Around her were droning electric engines, so smoothly balanced they seemed to be motionless as their giant flywheels spun at high velocity.

"This is a subsidiary power station," Quorne explained. He was alone now, his guards left behind to watch over Chris, Ethel and Barry. "You will notice two anode and cathode rods at either end of this power unit."

The Amazon looked at them and said nothing.

"Between them, at the throwing of a switch, energy can be made to leap—man-made lightning," Quorne explained. "That energy totally destroys whatever is in its path, particularly flesh and blood. If I suspend you between the globes and apply the power it will finish the matter—completely."

Quorne turned and pointed to the gallery above the power units. The Amazon began walking again, ascended the metal ladder, then proceeded along the narrow metal bridge that straddled the generators at a height of fifteen feet. When she was exactly halfway, Quorne called a halt. The Amazon turned and saw that he was holding a length of thin steel cable.

He considered the situation for a moment or two and then came forward. The Amazon stood passive as her ankles were wired tightly together, the wire passing up so that it secured her wrists immovably. She made no effort to break free—she was still incapable of exerting any will. In her mind was nothing but the crushing turmoil of hypnotic orders and the dim realization that death was coming—soon.

Quorne went back along the bridge to the gallery and brought another length of steel wire. He knotted it securely to the rail of the bridge. The free end of the wire he passed under the Amazon's arms in a noose, finishing with a slip knot. This done he knocked her feet from under her and then gave a push. She rolled over the edge of the bridge and dropped some ten feet, coming to a halt in mid-air as the steel wire drew taut. Gently she swung to and fro over the humming generators.

Quorne stood looking down on her for a moment, then he nodded in satisfaction and returned to the floor level. Moving to the switchboard, he gripped the insulated handle of a knife-blade switch.

"Sorry, Miss Brant," he called up to her swinging figure. "As I have frequently remarked, I admire you immensely, but in the game of power the weaker must be destroyed—"

And he slammed the switch home. Instantly there was a mighty upsurge in the whine of the generators. Livid tails of energy writhed between anode and cathode points, filling the air with crimping static. The Amazon vanished in a coruscation of blue-white sparks.

When the pyrotechnics were over, Quorne peered intently through the lavender-tinted haze. A steel wire hung from the bridge, one end curling up forlornly.

* * * * * * *

The Amazon was not dead.

In fact she did not know exactly what to think. As the energy had flashed across the gap where she had been helplessly hanging, something else had happened, too. It seemed as though the laboratory had exploded from before her eyes and now there were stars hurtling toward her with frightening velocity. Unbearable pressures crowded in upon her. Every nerve was twisted and racked.

She was sweeping through space, untouched by its virgin coldness, unhampered by the absence of air.

Stars, suns, nebulae rioted in front of her vision, yet she did not seem to have any physical eyes with which to see. Indeed, she was not conscious of her body at all. She was more like an anguished disembodied thought hurtling with the speed of light across infinity....

Then came a change. A feeling of life stole back into her limbs and with it movement ceased. She was breathing, but her hands and feet were immovable. Out of the obfuscation of her mind objects took shape. A laboratory again; huge machines; the archway of enormous magnets above her. Tubes glowing. She was lying flat on her back on a metal grid with an enormous young man in a toga-like costume looking down on her.

"Abna!" she whispered, then thought she must be dreaming.

She knew differently when without effort he swept her up in his arms and carried her to a soft couch. She said nothing as his powerful fingers snapped the steel wires apart. She still said nothing as he applied a healing ointment to her wounded shoulder and bandaged it.

"It is you, then?" she muttered at last, her violet eyes fixed on him.

"Naturally you're surprised?" he asked. "Or are you? I believe Chris and the rest of them went back to Earth. I expect they told you about me."

"Yes, they did, but—" The Amazon struggled up and looked about her in bewilderment. "This labora-tory—? Abna, am I on Jupiter?"

"You are," he assented calmly. "And here is our chaperone, since we're not married," he added drily.

The Amazon looked at the weird, stockily-built Jovian with his grey-scaled body. He was watching the proceedings with interest, a jar of ammoniated crystals clutched in one armadillo-like paw.

"You mean—?" The Amazon was still frowning.

"I mean, Vi, that I saved your life from Quorne. Not because I have any longer any regard for you after the way you ditched me on Io, but because we have to be together for common protection. I set a dissem-bler beam on the prison but found you had escaped; so I had to search for you again. I picked up your aura once more and by x-ray television saw that you were Quorne's captive, and he evidently was intending to kill you. Fortunately, I managed to pick you off with the dissembler beam just as Quorne released the energy upon you. My power being greater than his, it deflected the current, and, you were snatched away into space—to reassemble here in exactly the same way in which you had departed from Earth. Naturally you came here as an atomic parcel. The transformers reassembled you. You've made such a journey before: it ought not to be anything new to you."

"It isn't. I just wanted the facts, that's all."

The Amazon got to her feet and felt her bandaged shoulder. It already felt about normal again.

"All right," she said, shrugging. "So you brought me here on a business footing only. What's the business?"

"Quorne. But we can discuss it over a meal."

Abna made a signal and it stirred the lounging Jovian to life. He depressed a button on the nearby switchboard and a table rose out of the metal floor, supported on a broad pillar. Carried on radio beams, the meal appeared and settled in the correct positions on the table top. By the time Abna and the Amazon had seated themselves the meal was ready, consisting chiefly of essences.

Abna said: "In this Solar System, Vi, a triangle of power has come into being. You and I are at the base and, at the moment, Sefner Quorne is at the apex. I have to help you vanquish him before other worlds beside Earth go under his influence. The surest way to destroy him is to go to Earth and deal with him before he has gathered enough power to make an onslaught on me. So, I propose I help you smash his Earth control."

"I don't want your help, Abna."

Abna smiled. "You're not fooling me, Vi. I can read your mind, remember. You would have died in

Quorne's laboratory if I hadn't intervened. Even if you don't wish to be friendly any more, at least be honest."

"I don't wish to be deliberately unfriendly," she responded, after reflection. "You are too good a scientist to be ignored, Abna. Since I can't get rid of you, as I thought I had by stranding you on Io, I shall have to tolerate you, I suppose."

He smiled. "I understand why you threw me over. Apart from the fact that you wanted to learn all my secrets, you developed a fear that I might, in time, become more powerful than you. When you had learned my secrets, you threw me overboard."

"And you hurled me into furthest space!" the Amazon retorted. "I haven't forgotten that!"

"I blamed myself afterward," Abna muttered, frowning. "I ought to have used more restraint. However, you survived, and now were back where we started."

The Amazon snapped, "We are together, yes—as scientific partners only."

"Have you no intuitive ability to decide between love of me and love of power?" he asked.

"I don't love you. I made that clear long ago."

"In words, yes. But you can't alter your thoughts. You love me, Vi, and you're waging a perpetual war with yourself because of it."

She said nothing. In fact, she was not able, for Abna suddenly seized her in his arms and kissed her. She made an effort to break free, but her strength was not sufficient to break Abna's grip. He kissed her again.

"Don't take it so hard, Vi," he chuckled.

She blazed at him. "Abna—we're scientists! And you behave like a youth with his first love affair!"

"Why not? When a man loves a woman it's natural to kiss her. Why don't you break down and behave as though you're a human being?"

"Perhaps because I'm not," she answered slowly.

"Don't be ridiculous! You had a mother and a father—as I know from early inquiry about you—so that makes you human. Whatever else you may have acquired were caused by that scientist who did something to your gland structure."

She retorted: "When will you understand that Violet Ray Brant, a woman, is in complete subjection to the Golden Amazon, superwoman?"

"So that's it?" Abna asked, pondering. "If the superwoman no longer existed, you'd be amenable?"

There was a look in his eyes that the Amazon did not understand. It made her feel uneasy.

"What do you suppose happened to Chris, Ethel, and Barry?" Abna asked, changing the subject.

"We can find their aura-reading positions and then take a look with x-ray television," the Amazon responded; and with a nod Abna moved across to the instruments by the nearer wall. An hour later he and the Amazon had both satisfied themselves that the trio about whom they were concerned were still alive, back at duty in a space machine foundry, as before.

"Which destroys my plans completely," the Amazon sighed. "I had arranged for them to sabotage Quorne's work—as long as they were protected from hypnosis, of course—while I smashed up the brain-machine which is causing all the damage. Now they're slaves again and I am—"

"You are believed dead," Abna said. "I am sure Quorne believes his throwing of that master switch killed you. He would hardly be expecting me to throw a dissembler beam upon you at that identical moment. How much have you told him about me?"

"Nothing. He doesn't know whether you are alive or dead—but he does know our marriage wasn't genuine."

"He's right," Abna said. "Come over here, Vi: I want you to see my plan of attack."

She followed him across the huge laboratory. She had no idea where he was going—therefore it came as a complete surprise to her when he suddenly seized her shoulders and legs, whipped her from the floor, and deposited her on a long table they were passing. Before she could do a thing manacles snapped down over her wrists and ankles. A broader metal band clamped round her waist, and yet another at her throat. She lay immovable. She blinked as blinding light poured down on her from a cluster of shadowless arcs over the table.

"Abna," she panted, staring at him with wide eyes, "what is this? What are you—"

"I think it time I dissociated the woman from the superwoman," he answered. "You gave me the clue yourself. In your structure there is a makeup that stops you from ever being a human woman whom I might love and cherish. I love you enough, Vi, to destroy the Golden Amazon forever and make of her a plain woman, who shall become my queen, who will bring my race into being again and restore its past glories."

"Abna, you fool!" the Amazon shrieked, straining at the clamps. "What about Quorne? Your plan?"

"That can come later. It will not take me more than half an hour to operate on you. Reviving fluids will make you well again an hour from now. I've got to do it now. Then we can talk of Quorne."

"Abna, you don't know what you're doing! You must be insane!"

The Amazon's words smothered as the anaesthetic mask closed over her face. She struggled frantically in a smothering, strangling tide; then gradually the surroundings blanked out for her. Abna removed the mask, dipped his hands in a basin of cleansing fluid, then he turned to the case of instruments near the operating table. From the distances the Jovian came over to watch the proceedings.

With superb skill Abna went to work. He first shaved the Amazon's scalp and then trepanned the skull bone neatly with a thin ray. More electrical instruments with needle-like probes went to work on the Amazon's exposed brain until Abna was satisfied. Then he switched off and, under the glow of a healing blue beam, bone, hair, and tissue reformed.

Then he turned the Amazon on her face, ripped away the black tights down to her waist, then set to work on the glandular structure knitting to the spine. It was an operation that the most skilled Earth surgeon would never have dared to perform, involving as it did the alteration of nerve fibres and gland connections, as intricate as the wires in an involved electrical machine. But for Abna it had no terrors. He knew exactly what he was doing. His intimate knowledge of anatomy enabled him to see instantly where the long dead Dr. Axton, who had performed the experiment that had changed a normal girl into a superwoman, had switched the gland connections.

He finished his task, aware of the finality of the work. At length the flesh was reformed and left no trace of a scar. Unfastening the clamps, he raised the Amazon in one arm, supporting her shoulders, while with his free hand he drove a needle into the pulsing jugular on her neck. It drew a drop of blood that quickly vanished. Then she began breathing hard, reviving quickly under the powerful restorative surging through her bloodstream.

Abna smiled half to himself—not happily, but like a man who has done an unpleasant task thoroughly. He drew the torn tights into position at the back of the Amazon's neck and had just finished roughly securing them when she recovered consciousness. She looked about her, her violet eyes wide, then presently into his face.

"Better?" he inquired, smiling

"Yes," she agreed, frowning to herself. "Just what happened? I remember you— Why yes! You fastened me on this table and then—"

The Amazon stopped. She got slowly from the table

and stood upright. Abna regarded her intently.

"There's something wrong," she said. "I feel so utterly different. I haven't any energy, any alertness—Abna, what have you been doing to me?"

"Killing the Golden Amazon," he answered. "Just as I said I would."

"You mean you really did?" she asked, astounded.

He motioned her to follow him. Going to the nearest laboratory bench he picked up a metal bar and bent it swiftly in his hands; then he handed it to her. She took it and with a sudden effort tried to straighten the 'U' out. Instead she winced under the strain and the bar dropped to the floor.

"This happened to me once before," she whispered, her eyes aflame. "I lost my super-strength—but I got it back!"

"You won't this time, Vi. I've changed you back into the woman you should have been. You've only yourself to thank. If you had acceded earlier to my wishes this would have been unnecessary. As it is, I shall now have to think for both of us."

The Amazon turned away in anger. Abna followed her silently across the laboratory, his hand presently gripping her shoulder and forcing her to look at him.

"Don't you realize I have done all this because I love you?" he asked.

She shook her head dully. "You don't love me. Abna: I know it now more than I ever did. Your only concern is your race and the fact that I am a woman. Because I proved too clever for you, you took a mean advantage and robbed me of my strength and independence. Naturally you will do as you like with me because I have not the power to resist, but none of it will be with my willing consent."

"Your thoughts tell me you really mean that," he said slowly.

The Amazon smiled faintly. "Every word. You don't seem to realize that as the superwoman I had the intelligence to appreciate your genius as a scientist. As the ordinary woman I am now I have nothing but fear of you. I don't love you, Abna—not any more. And you have forgotten something else. One of your main aims in our intended marriage was the creation of superchildren. That could never happen now. One side of the genius has been wiped out—by you."

The Amazon withdrew slowly from Abna's grip and walked moodily to a nearby bench. Abna could not be sure of it, but he fancied when she glanced up that there were tears in her big violet eyes, the first tears he had ever seen there.

Abna turned away, his face grim. He thought for a moment and then unexpectedly met the stare of the yellow eyes of the Jovian, who shook his scaly head.

"That woman's no use, friend," his thoughts commented. "You could pick a million like her from Earth—none so beautiful maybe, but otherwise no different. You needed a Golden Amazon—not this."

"Keep your thoughts to yourself!" Abna snapped, so with a shrug the Jovian turned away, his gaze swinging across to where the Amazon was lounging morosely.

Presently Abna motioned to her. She came across to him and without a word he led the way to an affair rather like a gigantic electric organ manual, a small seat being screwed into the floor in the midst of banks of switches and numbered keys.

"This, Vi, is the apparatus which I hope will defeat Quorne," he said. "It is not necessary for us to fly across space with remote-controlled armadas in order to attack him. We can fight from here. This instrument controls heat beams, disintegrative radiation, four-dimensional vibrator—in fact, every weapon of attack known to Atlantean science. I can easily cover the distance to Earth with it, pinpointing the whole attack on that spot where the brain amplifier is located. The very suddenness of the onslaught should catch Quorne unawares and destroy him. Naturally, some Earth folk will die too, but it cannot be avoided. The point is to eliminate Quorne. Then we can turn around."

"I'll have to accept your word for everything," the Amazon answered. "I don't understand one thing about this apparatus."

"I don't expect you to. Your task will be to control the television apparatus so we can see where we are aiming. This is it, here."

"I don't understand that either," the Amazon said; then as Abna looked at her in startled wonder she added: "I'm not trying to be obstinate, Abna. I want Quorne destroyed as much as you do, but I can't help you. Everything scientific is a mystery to me."

Abna still gazed at her, his eyes perplexed. Then

she said: "As I remember it, you have a suite of rooms somewhere in this city that you put at my disposal when I was last here. I may as well change into something more womanly since the Amazon is dead."

She walked away across the laboratory and vanished beyond a massive bronze door. Abna compressed his lips and then flung himself in the chair before the scientific matrix. The Jovian drifted across to him.

"You've made a mistake, friend," he said. "Why not admit it? Of what possible use is that woman to you?"

"She's a woman, and I've the future of my race to think of," Abna snapped back. "Now leave me alone— or better still, you can handle the television. You may be lazy, but you're a first-class scientist."

"As you wish...." The Jovian settled before the instruments and tuned them in with his scaly paws. After a while a scene from 400-million mile distant London came into view. By working from the chart, the Jovian gradually altered focus until he had the squat building containing the brain amplifier dead-centred.

"Good enough," Abna acknowledged, and he closed the switches that brought power to the incredibly complicated mechanism he was operating. After a moment or two, during which the potential was building up, he snapped three more switches—then activated an indicator panel, exactly geared to the same focus reading as the television ray. With a vast upsurging of power from the generators a disintegrative beam hurtled across space toward Earth—and the brain amplifier building.

CHAPTER SEVEN
RESTORED TO NORMAL

Many minutes passed as the ray travelled. The Amazon returned to the scene of activity and Abna cast a glance at her. She was dressed in the rich garments of a woman of his race, a deep purple gown, sleeveless, with a brilliant orange sash about her waist.

"About as useful as a dummy," Abna growled in contempt, eyeing her. "Beautiful—and that's all. If I couldn't read your mind and know that you really do not understand science any more, I'd say you were trying to fool me."

"I'm only trying to fulfil the place you've set for me, Abna—to appear as and behave like an ordinary woman.... I assume you've started your attack?" she broke off, watching the screen.

Abna looked back at it quickly as the finger of the chronometer showed the time for the ray to reach Earth, and for the light images at the end of it to travel back was up. To the split second the brain amplifier building collapsed in a shattering chaos of dust and flame.

"That ends the brain amplifier," Abna commented, smiling in grim satisfaction. "Now I can follow up with these other beams before Quorne has a chance to—"

"A moment, friend," the Jovian interrupted, staring into the screen. "You've destroyed the building, but not the amplifier. It still stands!"

Abna, astounded, looked at the screen again. The Jovian was right. The big hemisphere encasing the ten brains was still standing untouched, and the switch panels around it did not appear to have suffered damage either.

"Quorne told me that apparatus is foolproof," the Amazon remarked. "Evidently he was right."

"I have other vibrations." Abna said fiercely, but before he could slam home the switches and release the full scientific fury of his attack there came a retaliating answer.

Obviously Quorne had been quick to realize he was being attacked, and undoubtedly with the instruments at his command it had not taken him above a few seconds to find where the source of the onslaught was situated. Whatever the explanation, his answer was immediate and devastating.

Out of the poisonous hurricane shielding Jove's surface there came the quivering roar set up by violent vibrational activity. It made the laboratory shake: then followed a tremendous report as far overhead the transparent dome covering the city cracked down its entire length. Abna stared up in alarm. As the vibration increased another part of the dome splintered.

"Quickly—the air chambers," he said, wheeling. "If the dome gives way, Vi, we'll be poisoned as the atmosphere comes in. The Jovian will be all right: it's natural fresh air to him. Quorne knows what this dome is made of and has the power to break it."

The din increased, then with a mighty roar part of the dome came hurtling down. The Amazon gave a hoarse cry as with a frantic effort Abna tried to hurl himself out of the way of that ten-ton mass of transparency hurtling down. He was not quick enough. It struck him, flattening him to the floor.

The Amazon looked about her helplessly—up at the greenish gas pouring in under the force of the exterior hurricane; then at Abna. She raced toward him and behind her another piece of the collapsing dome hit the floor.

"Abna!" she panted, going down on to her knees and tugging at his shoulders. "Abna—!"

He opened his eyes for a moment. The weight had fallen across him from the chest downward.

"No use, Vi," he whispered. "You could have saved me with your strength and surgical skill if I hadn't altered you. Maybe I deserved it. I—I could master this with—with my mind, if only I had—had time."

Pain contorted his face as he spoke. The Amazon looked at him helplessly, then jammed her bare shoulder against the shining side of the fallen substance. She shoved, but without avail. Formerly she could probably have raised the huge weight far enough for the nearby Jovian to drag Abna out.

"Abna—there's nothing I can do! If only—"

She stopped, the laboratory swimming wildly about

her as she drew in the first wisps of the poisonous atmosphere. She coughed violently, still looking at Abna's dead face—then the Jovian came hurtling across the floor. Before she knew what was happening the Amazon found herself dragged on her feet and, half-fainting with the gas, she was bundled into a spacesuit and had the helmet slammed down over her head. The air supply worked instantly and slowly her head cleared.

The dome, smashed in three places, was open to the tumult of the Jovian hurricane. The Amazon could hear it screaming in the suit's audiophones—then came more trouble as in a haze of deep red—a heat beam—the more distant instruments and pillars began to melt into plasma. Evidently Quorne was intent on complete destruction.

"What do we do?" the Amazon asked, staring through her helmet at the Jovian as, unaffected by the ammoniated hydrogen, he gazed about him.

Her thoughts back of the question reached him and his telepathic answer was immediate.

"I can stay here, Earth woman, but you cannot. I must return you to your own world."

"But how? Look at the machines—they're being smashed in all directions."

"I cannot do it by instantaneous transportation, even though I understand the principle," the Jovian said. "I shall have to fly you there in a space machine. Unless you can pilot yourself?"

The Amazon shook her head dumbly, so the Jovian

grabbed her gloved hand and hurried her across the laboratory away from the immediate area being destroyed. He knew where the space machines were housed, and he entered the area in which were stored half a dozen vessels. The Amazon had just time to survey them when the lighting failed with the annihilation of the generators. So she submitted to the grip of the Jovian's scaly paw and eventually found herself within a control room as roof lamps sprang into being. The Jovian released her, clamped the airlock shut, then settled at the control-panel.

"The power being off," he said, "I shall have to smash through the roof. Then I can drive through one of the dome cracks and into outer space."

The Amazon nodded, understanding his thoughts, and sank down on the wall couch heavily. Power surged into the generators under the movement of a switch: they in turn supplied the power to the rockets. Then the machine, smaller by far than the mighty *Ultra*, hurtled upward, crashed through the roof as though it did not exist, and for a while buzzed around in the darkness immediately under the dome—but always keeping clear of that dim red radiance still smashing the city into dust.

Then out into space, shooting through the green vapours of the atmosphere, riding the eternal hurricane. Onward, upward, faster and faster, until at last free space was gained.

The Amazon stood up, took off her space suit, then relaxed again. She was trying to absorb the bewildering fact that she had no scientific knowledge left. She was completely in the hands of the queer, loyal being whose crocodile-like back was turned toward her as he studied the screens.

And Abna? Back there on Jupiter, crushed under the weight of smashed machines? The Amazon closed her eyes at the thought. It began to look as though the whole effort to destroy Sefner Quorne had ended in a grim debacle and left him the master of the situation.

"You expect destruction, Earth woman, when you arrive back on your planet?" the Jovian questioned.

"Obviously," she answered. "My features are unchanged. I'm going right back to death, Jovian."

"No," he said. "This machine, like your *Ultra*, is proof against such hypnosis. As for when we arrive on Earth—well, there may be a way."

The Amazon studied his hideous face. "Tell me, Jovian, why take these risks for my sake?"

The hideous grin cracked the Jovian's face. "The Jovians are wanderers, and I have long wanted to see other worlds. If I do you a good turn as well, all the better. I like helping people: I feel it compensates for being such a sluggard in other things."

"A genius with feet of lead," the Amazon smiled. "That is what you are, Jovian."

"Possibly. I understand science, even as you once did—even as you will again," he finished.

"Not again," she answered, sighing. "Abna made too good a job of things for that."

The Jovian took a long drink of nitric acid and

pondered for a moment, but whatever was in his mind he did not utter it. Instead he came back to the problems that would arise when Earth was reached.

"Your mind tells me, Earth woman, that you have secret laboratories at various points on your planet. Can we not go to one of them?"

"Easily—granting we ever get past the patrols who attack any newcomer to Earth. They will know me as the Golden Amazon."

"Sefner Quorne believes he killed you, and your whole manner is so different that you might be mistaken for a woman who only resembles the Amazon. Why not call yourself a traveller from Mars? Quorne has not yet conquered that world or even attempted to. Pass yourself off as a stranger, and see what happens. You may be permitted to go through. I'll stay in hiding."

The Amazon looked at her flowing robes and shrugged.

"I can try, but I don't expect much. One thing will always give me away—my aura. Quorne will know me by that."

"We'll try and reach one of your secret laboratories if we can," the Jovian decided, "but should events separate us you may rely on me to keep watch over you somehow. I can read from your mind where your laboratories are, so I'll surely find one of them."

Her gratitude—a virtue she had never possessed before—went out to him for his loyalty.

When the space flyer came within range of Earth, a group of interceptor machines came toward it.

"I'll stop the machine and then hide," the Jovian said, and gave a blast to the forward rockets that slowed down the vessel's velocity.

By the time the interceptors came level, the Jovian had his vessel almost motionless. He gave an encouraging grip on the Amazon's arm and departed quickly to the storage locker and shut himself in.

The machines grouped about her. A tube was projected from the nearest machine's airlock to the airlock of her vessel and a voice on the radio ordered her to unlock the doors. She obeyed. Three guards came along the sealed tube and into the control-room.

It was plain from their expressions that they received a considerable shock as they gazed at her; then the foremost got control of himself. His gun ready for use he took a few steps toward her.

"Name and business?" he asked briefly.

"I'm travelling from Mars—Emerson City," the Amazon answered. "I have relatives on Earth and not having heard from them for a time I'm getting worried. My name is Drexel. Fay Drexel."

"The inhabitants of Earth are no longer able to communicate with other planets," the guard said brusquely. "Under the new regime instituted by Sefner Quorne, all Earthlings are fitted into a master plan. Drexel, you say? You have identity papers?"

"Not with me. I never thought I'd need them. I never have before."

One of the three guards said: "I'd suggest she be given an insulation helmet and that we let Quorne see her. He might even find her useful. Her resemblance to the Golden Amazon is astounding."

The Amazon laughed regretfully. "I've been told that before. I'm afraid it ends in mere resemblance, though. What is all this mystery you're talking about—Sefner Quorne and a new regime?"

"Those on Mars are not yet acquainted with the facts," the guard said. "You will be in good time. Take over," the guard added to one of his colleagues. "Fly this machine to Earth—Quorne's headquarters. And you, Miss Drexel, wear this on your head, please."

She took from him the fine metal skullcap he handed over. She recognized it immediately as the type of insulated cap she herself had invented, though in this case it was without the wig. With a vague wonder as to how she had ever conceived such an idea, she fitted the cap into place and the guard gave a nod.

"Don't remove that until instructed," he said. "It is to protect you against powerful hypnosis beams existing on Earth."

The Amazon said nothing, so the guard departed with one colleague, leaving the other behind to fly the machine to Earth. For this the Amazon was thankful; it meant she did not have to admit that she had not the least idea how to operate the vessel.

In an hour the machine touched Earth, settling in the large grounds surrounding a London building that Quorne had evidently made his headquarters. The Amazon's last thought, as she left the vessel, was for the Jovian in the storage chamber. She wondered how he would fare—or if she would ever see him again.

She was escorted into a huge room that had the appearance of a highly scientific office. In all directions there were panels and switchboards, and the main desk at which Sefner Quorne himself was seated was studded with buttons.

He looked up as the guards entered, then his heliotrope eyes became fixed on the Amazon. She walked with her usual queenly dignity, an inborn characteristic, the long robes trailing behind her.

"You!" Quorne breathed, rising. "Miss Brant!"

"No, sir," the leading guard said. "She says her name is Fay Drexel and that she's a traveller from Mars. We picked her up on the incoming journey. Routine type space machine."

"You are Miss Brant!" Quorne snapped. "I couldn't be so mistaken. I admit it is a surprise because I thought I had destroyed you, but—"

"You are not alone in being misled as to my identity, sir," the Amazon said quietly. "My resemblance to her has often been remarked."

"Resemblance? You are the Amazon! And I can soon prove it."

He took a small compass-like instrument from his desk and directed the pointer toward her. She knew perfectly well that her aura was being determined, and that, as far as she could see, was the finish of everything. But to her amazement Quorne looked at her in wonder.

"I apologize, Miss Drexel," he said. "If you were

the Amazon, your aura number would tally with this compass, a method as infallible as fingerprints used to be. Since your aura is many degrees different, I admit I have been mistaken."

"It is understandable," the Amazon replied, smiling. It occurred to her that the change made in her bodily structure by Abna had also changed her former all-devouring energy, hence the aura was altered.

Quorne motioned and dismissed the guards, then he drew up a chair and waited while the Amazon seated herself.

"I have the feeling, Miss Drexel, that you may be of invaluable assistance to me, having such a resemblance to the Amazon. She, in case you are not aware of it, is dead."

"Oh? I have had no news of any kind on Mars, sir. I don't understand what is happening on Earth here. My relatives are—"

"I am controlling Earth, Miss Drexel—and working to a master plan. For the sake of convenience every inhabitant is controlled hypnotically. Later I will see that you are permitted to speak to your relatives. Meantime, you escape this hypnosis because of that cap you are wearing."

The Amazon nodded. It also prevented her thoughts being read.

"Yes," Quorne mused, "you are identical to the late Amazon in every way. Yellow-skinned, violet-eyed, golden haired— Your yellow skin? How do you account for it?"

"My father was of Mongolian extraction," the Amazon said, and this seemed to satisfy Quorne for he nodded. Then he continued:

"My plans as far as this planet are concerned are complete, but very shortly I intend to take Mars under my control. It is possible the colonists there will resent it. But that would not happen if you smoothed the path for me. That is, you would present yourself to them as the Golden Amazon and announce that you have pooled your resources with mine. You understand?"

"You think I would be capable of it?" the Amazon asked.

"I'm sure you would be. In fact, Miss Brant, after your monumental courage in presenting yourself to me as Fay Drexel, I am willing to believe you can do anything."

The Amazon looked up sharply. Quorne was standing by the desk, his purple eyes fixed on her face, his gun in his hand.

"I have been talking nonsense, Miss Brant," he said drily. "I was merely taking the time to study you. Now I am satisfied. Despite having changed your aura radiation—even as I have changed mine—you are the Golden Amazon. Yet somehow I admit you are changed in manner. Less—er—volatile, shall I say?"

"You are entitled to say what you like," the Amazon answered moodily. "As to my having the courage to come here—I didn't. I was brought."

"I know you are the Amazon for the simple reason that when I attacked Jupiter, in response to the attack on me, I had television beams on the planet to see where I was striking. I saw you—in the self-same gown you are wearing now—and Abna, and somebody else who looked like a Jovian. After that, smoke and dust hid the view, so I don't know what occurred. Presumably you came directly to Earth with some kind of fantastic plan to deceive me. How did you escape?"

"Does it matter? I did escape, Quorne. But Abna did not. You killed him when you attacked Jupiter."

"I did?" Quorne's eyes gleamed. "That is excellent news. I have only you left to deal with then. One thing I must know. How did you change your aura? I thought it was my secret alone."

The Amazon was silent. Quorne's hand shot out and gripped her wrist tightly, his other hand holding his gun. He was not attempting to hurt her, but evidently he did, for she winced under his steel clutch.

"What is this?" he asked. "The Amazon wilts like a weak woman under a mere pressure of the fingers?" He suddenly transferred his grip to her upper arm and dragged her out of the chair. With an easy movement he sent her spinning' against the desk where she remained, breathing hard, fear in her eyes.

Quorne relaxed, grinning at her.

"So we face an interesting situation," he murmured. "You are not playing a part, Miss Brant. I know fear when I see it. You are frightened—and weak! And I think I know why. Abna brought this about. He performed some kind of surgical experiment which changed your energy quotient."

He snatched the skullcap from her head and immediately the iron grip of compulsion was holding her mind. She did not know exactly what happened, but she was aware of being bundled into the radius of a machine that directed a beam at her head. Its probing bit through the haze of other thoughts in her mind: then the cap was replaced on her head. Quorne was looking quietly triumphant.

"Very satisfactory, Miss Brant," he announced. "Unfortunately your present state of mind makes it impossible for me to learn any scientific secrets. But I have been able to read that you have been reduced to the level of an ordinary woman, that Abna definitely is dead, and that you came to Earth through the assistance of a Jovian—whom I shall make it my business to destroy, even as I intend to destroy you. I don't propose to take any more risks in regard to you, even though at the moment you are quite innocuous—"

Quorne broke off end twirled round sharply as the door of his office suddenly flew open. His expression changed at the vision of three guards making desperate efforts to restrain a squat, scaly figure with a helmet strapped over his crocodile-like head. They might as well have tried to stop a whirlwind.

To the Jovian's superhuman strength, multiplied by the fact that he was accustomed to Jupiter's huge gravity instead of the slight pull of Earth, the guards were mere encumbrances. With one fling of his power-packed arm he dashed the nearer guard senseless against the wall; the second he threw across the office and clear through the big window; the third he squeezed to death with one clutch of his scaly paw round the throat. Then he came forward on his block-like legs.

If he said anything by telepathy it was not apparent, his helmet negated all outflowing waves. But Quorne acted, recovering from his first astonishment. He fired his gun point blank, but the ray it projected glanced off the armoured hide and made no impression. The Jovian kept moving, bleak murder in his yellow eyes. Quorne gave an alarmed look about him, then he grabbed at the nearby Amazon and put her in front of him as a shield.

With one arm the Jovian encircled the Amazon's waist and swung her up on to his shoulder, dragging her clear of Quorne's grasp. With his free paw he seized Quorne's throat and crushed hard—but Quorne tore himself out of the steel clutch and raced across to his switchboard.

The Jovian hesitated, uncertain as to what would happen next. Then he swung around and headed out at top speed the way he had come, the Amazon still dangling over his shoulder. In the hallway were guards. They fired at him without effect, but two of the rays struck the Amazon and burned livid slashes across her back. She found her senses beginning to swim under the pain of the burns.

In a confused fashion she realized the Jovian had borne her to the outside of the building, and that he was fighting his way by sheer titanic strength through more guards. Then he leaped easily in the light gravity and landed on top of the wall encircling the grounds of the headquarters.

To the Amazon the sense of confusion deepened, and gradually faded into oblivion as the burning pain in her back increased. Her next awareness was of tinkling sounds like faraway bells. She opened her eyes slowly, shut them again at the brilliance of light that struck her, then opened them once more.

The tinkling was the sound of the Jovian putting gleaming instruments back into a glass-sided case. He was standing looking at her, his hideous face as near concerned as it could be, his yellow eyes intent. He was without his helmet now and this brought the Amazon to feeling at her own head. She, too, had lost her protective cover. It also occurred to her that her flowing robes had gone and she was nearly naked.

For some reason she did not feel embarrassed by the thought. The Jovian was a scientist of another world entirely. To him she was not a woman but a female of an alien species. Then he handed her a very civilized-looking dressing gown, and she draped it about her as she slid from the long table on which she had been lying.

"Better?" came the Jovian's anxious inquiry.

She looked at him and then considered herself. Energy, vital and surging, was flowing through her veins. All the apathy and weakness she had possessed before had vanished.

"What happened?" she questioned.

"I operated on you. I had to. You were nearly cut

in two by those ray burns. Apart from repairing that damage, I restored your internal structure to the position it was in before Abna interfered, and I reconnected your brain where Abna had severed a nerve that prevented you from remembering your scientific achievements. You are the Golden Amazon again."

She said nothing. The faculty of gratitude had left her. Going over to the instrument case, she took her temperature and examined her reflexes and blood pressure, then with a grim smile of satisfaction she returned to where the Jovian was standing watching her.

"This is a tremendous achievement on your part, friend," she said. "How did you manage it?"

"Simple," came his thoughts. "I saw Abna perform the original operation; it was not difficult to reverse the process. You were never meant to be an ordinary woman, Amazon. You are the first of the superwomen.... I found this London laboratory of yours after a good deal of interference from guards, and once I'd got here, the rest was easy. I found where the generators were and started them up, blanketing the outside of the laboratory with a radiation-shield so hypnotic power cannot affect us."

"Good work. This is my central London laboratory—and before long I assume that Quorne will attack it. I'm not quite clear what happened to him— You didn't kill him?"

"No. I wasn't sure how much power he was intending to release on me, and your safety came first. When you left your spaceship, I made myself a protective helmet from the ship's equipment and came after you. You were not in any fit state then to be left to your own devices."

"Very true," the Amazon admitted. "And, of course, Quorne knows we are here?"

"Possibly so by now. I fought his guards until the last moment—but it's just possible I shook them off before coming down here. I don't have to tell you this laboratory of yours is half a mile underground, and protected by three energy barriers in the downshaft. Even Quorne won't find it easy to penetrate this far— and the energy shield around the laboratory proper should block him."

The Amazon nodded, reflected for a moment, and then said:

"Prepare a meal for us, Jovian, while I change."

His scaly head nodded. It did not signify in the least to him that in spite of the scientific work he had done he was being treated with no more respect than a servant. He expected it. In fact, it pleased him: nothing could have convinced him more that the Earth-woman was the intellectual and physical giantess she had formerly been.

CHAPTER EIGHT
COUNTER ATTACK

She went to the quarters of the laboratory given over to living use, and returned in her skin-tight black suit, a new golden belt of instruments about her waist, her hair caught back by a gleaming band studded with rubies. The Jovian had prepared a meal, and she commenced eating. The Jovian's thoughts did not interrupt her; he was busy with his own extraordinary meal of ammoniated crystals and a jar of nitric acid.

"At the moment," the Amazon said presently, "the situation is that Sefner Quorne is still on top—and he has destroyed one corner of the power triangle by killing Abna. We have been driven underground, leaving him as undisputed master."

The Jovian said: "Quorne has no idea that you have gained your strength and power once again. He is unable to reach you here, and he is in the dark as to where you will strike next, as of course I suppose you intend to?"

The Amazon clenched her yellow fist on the table. "I shall break his hold on Earth, Jovian, if it is the last thing I do. Since it seems that all known radiations are powerless against that ten-brain amplifier, there is only one other course to pursue—use the scientific fact that any living object, for remember those brains do live, must die in its own waste."

It was clear from the Jovian's thoughts that he was puzzled, so the Amazon outlined more elaborately.

"A breathing creature dies in the waste of its own exhalation if it be sealed in," she explained. "These brains do not breathe, but they emit a torrent of pooled thoughts. One thing would surely destroy that unit—to have its thoughts reflected back on itself with 100-fold power."

"Scientifically correct," the Jovian agreed, "but it will tax your scientific ingenuity to the full to find a means of reflecting the thoughts waves to—"

"The means already exists," the Amazon interrupted. "In remote space there is a planetoid which is a natural reflector of thought. I encountered it when Abna hurled me into infinity. I was nearly driven insane by the reflection and echo of my own thoughts. The effect would be infinitely more frightful on amplified brain waves: it would burn the brains out completely, I think, and bring Quorne and all his works to a standstill. To ever find this incredibly distant planetoid again by ordinary searching would be impossible, but it so happens that I removed a section of it for examination —the merest fragment, of course. It is not so much a planetoid as a living creature of low thought-order, made up of mineral and organic tissue. Now, any organic tissue has an aura radiation, the same as any living thing. That fragment will give me the aura-number, and a super-powerful aura compass, which I shall have to construct, will show me exactly where the planetoid lies, and its distance away."

"Agreed," the Jovian responded, finding no fault so far. "Then what? You are not suggesting you drag an entire planetoid out of its orbit, are you?"

"Yes." the Amazon answered decisively. "If I can locate this planetoid, I intend to handle it by push-and-pull beams—repulsion and attraction, that is—manoeuvre it through four-dimensional space until it comes to rest in the same position where I found myself when I catapulted myself out of deep space to a spot quite near Earth. I already have the four-dimensional equations necessary to that operation—as far as the actual movement is concerned. They will have to undergo modifications because of the size of the body now involved."

"You mean that using the fourth dimension will obviate delay in the planetoid crossing space?"

"Exactly—space can be foreshortened. Further, it will avoid the conflicting drag of the giant outer planets in trying to pull the planetoid Earthwards into the inner solar system. There will be no opposition in the fourth dimension. Put more plainly, this reflective planetoid must be transplanted from one position in space to another, by means of utilizing hyperspace—which, technically, is the fourth dimension. Even at that, it may take many months to accomplish the feat so prodigious is the distance. But I believe it can be done, granting the planetoid is not beyond all reach of a compass. I once rekindled the sun from Mercury, and I don't regard this as more difficult."

The Jovian's thoughts came presently: "Where is this sample of the planetoid?"

"Aboard my *Ultra*, in its laboratory. And the *Ultra* is in my Cornwall retreat, ninety miles from here. It will mean we must go there—somehow. Further, to put the whole plan into operation, we can't work from Earth here: Quorne would smash us before we could even start. My suggestion is that we work from Pluto, on the very rim of our solar system."

"I see from your mind that there are other minor planets even more distant—and therefore nearer to the planetoid."

"True, but their composition is still largely unknown. Pluto we have studied with unmanned probes and we know it is a stable, rocky body of almost the same mass as Earth. It will make a good base for the purpose I have in mind."

"Wherever you go, friend, I am willing to go," the Jovian responded. "As I once told you, I like to wander."

The Amazon said, grasping his scaly paw in her yellow fingers: "Let us consider ourselves partners, Jovian. You are one after my own heart—unbonded and free, a good scientist, and immensely strong. We can work well together, you and I."

"I am a poor substitute for Abna," came his thoughts.

"I disagree. As far as you are concerned, I can never be physically attracted toward you, any more than you can toward me. Which makes for the ideal combination. Yes, Pluto," the Amazon continued. "I've never yet been there. That little world beyond Neptune should make a good base of operations. First, though, we have to reach Cornwall without being observed."

"Ninety miles," the Jovian mused. "There is one way to do it without being seen—instantaneous transportation. Dissembly of our atoms at this end and their recreation at the destination."

"Exactly—which you read from my mind," the Amazon said; then she got to her feet and added: "We had better be on our way."

The Jovian accompanied her across the laboratory to the area between two enormous magnets, which formed the basis of the atomic transporter—a painful but sure way of projecting a living or inanimate object across a distance and causing it to reassemble at the limit of the projected beam.

For a while the Amazon was busy calculating the exact position of her Cornish hideout, measuring on the scale map and then adjusting the instruments on the transporter itself. Finally she was satisfied, and threw the switches that set the power coursing through the apparatus. Another switch killed the lights of the laboratory itself, then as a dim, shadowy figure she joined the Jovian on the transmission plate and waited.

After a while there came the ghastly sensation to which she was inured, but which was a new sensation to the Jovian. His thoughts showed the pain he was experiencing as his body was dissolved into its atomic composition alongside the Amazon—then for both of them, came that reeling certainty of headlong falling through endless dark until the threads were taken up again.

When they materialized, they were in darkness and the Amazon said: "If my calculations are right, we should be in the centre of my Cornish laboratory."

She moved with her uncanny faculty for penetrating darkness and found a cold-light switch that snapped under her groping hand and a dazzling blaze of light opened up.

"This is a far better laboratory, friend, than the other one," came the Jovian's thoughts.

"I consider it my best one," the Amazon answered.

He watched with interest as she fashioned an instrument. A transparent dome was formed, then a small and faultlessly balanced spindle, and finally a needle upon the end of which glittered diamond dust.

"Aura compass?" he questioned, and the Amazon nodded.

"Yes. With which to trace that planetoid. This is the most sensitive long-distance compass I've yet made."

When it was finished, she brought from the *Ultra* the fragment of the unknown planet. She laid it between two magnetic readers and threw the current. The dial said 67987.

"Aura number," the Amazon explained. "A human being's aura number rarely goes beyond four figures: this time we have five, a not unexpected occurrence when dealing with a planetoid. Our task now is to set the compass to the same figure and see if we get a reaction."

The needle spun aimlessly in its vacuum case, wavered, and then became steady. The Amazon peered at it, her violet eyes gleaming.

"It works, Jovian!" she breathed. "Look at that! Colossal though the distance must be, the needle reacts— Now to calculate the distance."

She pressed the oscillator button and the needle started to rock up and down. At the same time the computer linked to the compass began to check the number of swings and work out in equations the distance of the object concerned.

Never in all her career had the Amazon had to wait so long for a distance to be read. She walked about the laboratory in nervous impatience while the more stolid Jovian watched the needle with fascinated interest. An hour passed, two hours, three hours, and the needle was still swinging, though with slightly less impetus. Four and a half hours after its initial swing, it came to rest and the Amazon snatched the calculated reading from the computations.

"A great distance is right," she said, with a low whistle as the Jovian watched her. "That hell planetoid—as I call it—is eleven thousand million miles away, or about three times the distance of Pluto!

For a moment there was silence as the incomprehensible expanse of space was digested, then the Amazon came back to action with her usual air of decision.

"At least we know what we have to do," she said.

"We will equip the *Ultra* with every needful machine tool, although it has a fair supply already, and then set out for Pluto. We'll take extra copper blocks, too. I don't intend to run out of fuel this time. You can give me a hand to move all the necessary equipment. Incidentally, you have a name, Jovian?"

"As near as I can interpret it into your language, Amazon, it is Relka," he responded.

"Relka it shall be henceforth," the Amazon pronounced, then she indicated the machine-tool equipment she required transporting. And in this particular task the huge strength of the Jovian against the lightness of Earth gravity was a decided asset.

A few hours later the *Ultra* was fully stocked, not only with equipment but provisions and spare power-blocks. Satisfied with her final check-over, the Amazon closed the doors of her laboratory and then moved the time-switch which caused the cliff face to open. Entering the *Ultra*'s control-room, she settled at the instrument panel and drove the monster vessel out into the darkness. Behind her the cliff face resealed automatically.

"Apparently Quorne has no idea what we're doing," came the Jovian's thoughts, as he peered into the summer dusk. "Otherwise he'd have been attacking by now."

"Not through barriers of energy," the Amazon answered. "He isn't such a fool. And those barriers would prevent my aura being read, too. Granting he tried. Perhaps now he believes it changed, he wouldn't bother."

She closed the power switches, and the central plant hummed as the massive copper block began to disintegrate imperceptibly. The *Ultra* quivered, then without perceptible motion swept up from the rocky ground and hurtled toward the misty stars.

Knowing that she and the Jovian could both stand the strain, she did not hesitate to give the vessel full acceleration—and in a matter of minutes they flashed through the troposphere and stratosphere and out into space. Instantly the mist was gone from the stars and they blazed in frigid glory, packed in a tight diamond dust and reaching depth upon depth into inconceivable distance.

"This is where we can expect trouble," the Amazon said, still slowly building up the speed. "As we cross the alarm-belt ringing space near Earth, Quorne will have an idea what has happened when no vessel comes toward Earth. His telescopes should show us streaking away into the void, and unless I'm mistaken he'll come chasing us."

"We can deal with it, if so," the Jovian responded.

But for some reason or other the Amazon's expectations were not realized. The orbit of the Moon was passed, and there was still no sign of pursuit. The orbit of Mars was left behind; then that of the asteroids; and giant Jupiter loomed once more. The Amazon considered it with an unwonted air of sadness as the *Ultra*—keeping well away from the huge gravity field—streaked onward.

"Abna?" the Jovian's thoughts questioned, as he saw her expression.

Her golden head nodded. "I shall never cease to think, Relka, that Abna and I completely misunderstood one another from the first. Each of us powerful; each of us unwilling to give way. However, it is over now. He is gone and I am left."

With an air of unalterable decision, she turned back to the controls, and gradually Jupiter passed by and the looming gap to magnificent Saturn was crossed at the same stupendous rate. Saturn of the rings, most superb astronomical architecture in the System. The Amazon contemplated the planet as it loomed ahead and she gave a thoughtful smile.

"Relka, I have that world yet to explore," she said. "As well as Uranus and Neptune. I've long had the ambition to bring every planet in the System under Earth control, and someday I will—you and I together maybe. Pluto perhaps may also be useful to us—apart from it being our base of operations for this present campaign."

"And my own planet Jupiter?" Relka answered. "Do you consider that now falls under Earth dictate?"

"Most certainly—or it will when Quorne is disposed of. Jupiter's Atlantean settlement can be turned into a thriving city for settlers if a new dome is built."

"It is a pity all the machines were destroyed. We might have used them in our present plan."

On and still on. The gap to Saturn was covered eventually, and the lovely—from a distance—planet left far behind. More endless hours of sleep and waiting. The orbit of Uranus passed—then Neptune—until there only remained the small mass of remote Pluto in the depths ahead, and beyond him the glittering expanses of intergalactic space.

"Not far to go now," the Amazon said, happy at the thought of perhaps being able to escape the imprisoning walls of the *Ultra*, even if only in a spacesuit. "A matter of only a few million miles to Pluto—I've often wondered what kind of a world he is," she broke off. "Always struck me as being the black sheep of the Solar System. Smaller by far than the neighbouring giants—indeed not really a planet at all—yet stacked densely enough to have a gravity not a great deal less than Earth. Following a crazy orbit that brings him nearer to the sun than Neptune sometimes. Yes, an odd world. Our own readings on it show him frozen solid."

Relka did not respond. He was watching the remote outpost as it came nearer through the infinity of space. Then he glanced rearward to where the sun had so enormously decreased in size that it appeared no more than a first-magnitude star. Out here in these lonely wastes there was only a tiny fraction of the sun's light and heat compared to that on Earth.

To bring the *Ultra* down to Pluto's surface was a simple task for the Amazon. He had no atmosphere to make vision difficult, hence no clouds. His mountain ranges were low and rambling after the fashion of giant Jupiter. Though it was the Plutonian day, the sun just an extra bright star in the hosts of heaven; it looked about as light on the Plutonian landscape as two in the morning reflected on a starry night on Earth.

Not a thing moved, not a thing lived. Stark, barren rock held solid in the grip of inconceivable space-zero.

"Gravity somewhat less than Earth," the Amazon announced, studying the instruments. "Humidity and atmospheric content are practically zero. They don't exist to any real extent. Temperature, minus 230 degrees centigrade, which is not far from absolute zero. Not exactly a happy world to come to, Relka, but an excellent outpost nonetheless."

The Jovian brought the spacesuits from the storage locker. Although his normal atmosphere of Jupiter was mainly ammoniated hydrogen, his fantastic metabolism enabled him to adapt to breathe the same air as the Amazon. Then, carrying instruments and equipment, he and the Amazon stepped out through the safety lock onto the surface and began their lonely journey over the plain. Behind them the *Ultra* was ablaze with light, so they could not fail to return to it, and for extra precaution, thin wire uncoiled from their suits as they went, fastened to the *Ultra*'s prow.

Because of the relative smallness of Pluto, the horizon seemed far nearer than a similar distance on Earth, the blaze of stars sweeping down to its very edge. The two went on for perhaps a couple of miles, then the Amazon led the way to a high eminence. "This tableland up here will be a good spot from which to operate your apparatus," Relka said. "You have a complete view of infinity."

"Excellent spot," the Amazon responded, and her thoughts carried her words. "We may as well—"

She broke off in amazement, and at the same instant Relka gripped her arm. In complete incredulity they watched the distant *Ultra*, portholes ablaze, leaping up and sweeping high above their heads.

"Quorne!" the Amazon cried, and began running—but the spacesuit hampered her movements. Then suddenly she was whirled from her feet as the guide wire attached to the belt about her waist reeled out to the limit. She swung helplessly in space, being whisked ever higher toward the stars. To her rear she caught a glimpse of Relka being dragged likewise.

The Amazon swung herself in the void until she had caught hold of Relka, then clutching him she spoke—and as usual her thoughts reached him.

"I cannot imagine anybody else but Quorne doing this," she said, "but obviously he didn't know about these guide wires. We'll climb up them when we are far enough from Pluto for his gravity not to worry us. That will mean that the only mass to attract us will be the *Ultra* itself. We can get to it that way and walk round it to the summit. To fall off will be impossible, because it will be the only field of attraction. And there is a secret trapdoor on the *Ultra*'s summit that only I know about. I think we can get inside and deal with Quorne—for the last time."

With that the Amazon swung away again and the dizzying ascent to the stars continued. It was the kind of nightmare flight that would have killed any ordinary being from sheer vertigo—but not the Amazon, accustomed to the vagaries of space and falling through bottomless distances. She remained motionless on the end of the wire, its strength and the belt about her waist the only safeguard against falling many miles back to receding Pluto.

Then after a time the Amazon realized that her heavy metal-shod feet were slowly moving upward. Those boots, the heaviest part in her spacesuit, were turning gradually to a new force of attraction as Pluto's grip weakened—the *Ultra* above her. Pluto by now was so far away, he was becoming a negligible quantity as far as gravity was concerned. Neptune would be the next trouble, but he was still many millions of miles distant.

So, very gradually, the Amazon found her feet drawn irresistibly upward as gravity changed position. By ordinary standards she was finally upside down, but not according to gravity. The *Ultra* had become a tiny planet and at whatever point she stood on it she was as upright as though walking the Earth itself.

She looked across at Relka who, likewise, had turned completely over—then she signalled him. Setting the example she hauled herself with supreme ease up the wire until her feet struck the *Ultra*'s underside gently. To fall off was impossible: it would only mean she would float back. So she began walking carefully over the massive armour plate—first apparently upside down, then horizontal, and finally upright as she came to the summit. From her own point of view she had been upright all the time with the stars circling around her in her movement.

Taking care to make no noise in case it carried through the plates to the control room she crept along to the secret exterior lock, operated the combination bolt through her thick gloves, then lowered herself gently into a dark cavity. In a moment or two Relka followed her, clamping the airlock shut behind her. They waited until air pressure automatically filled the safety lock in which they stood—then the second valve opened and gave them a view of the control room below, seen through the metal network of a removable ventilation grid.

CHAPTER NINE
CAUGHT IN A TRAP

The figure at the control board, his back turned, was undoubtedly Sefner Quorne. She nodded to Relka and then took off her helmet and unpeeled the space suit. She waited until the Jovian was ready also, and then by slow degrees began removing the ventilator grille immediately above Quorne's head.

Once he glanced about him as though he heard something, then he returned his attention to the controls. The Amazon's gaze settled on his gun on the bench beside him. There remained the obvious course—to shoot him dead before he even had a chance to know what had hit him, but this the Amazon was reluctant to do, not from any merciful considerations, but because her scientific curiosity was aroused. She was baffled as to how Quorne had beaten her, and wanted the answer.

She hesitated. Threatening him with her own gun would be useless. He'd risk everything and flash up his own gun and fire. If she tried dropping through the gap on top of him he'd have momentary warning from the noise and act first.

"One way only," the Amazon murmured, "if I'm

ever to batter the truth out of him without getting killed myself...."

She silently removed the ventilator grille so a wide space loomed. Intent on his screens and instruments, Quorne did not notice anything.

"I'll leap on him," the Amazon murmured to Relka. "I can move so fast he'll never know what hit him."

She was right. One moment Quorne was studying figures on the instruments—the next something with the fury of a wild beast landed on his back. His hand flew to his gun but a merciless grip on his wrist tore his arm upward and backward. Another arm crushed under his jaw and he was dragged back from the control chair.

He landed finally on the metal floor and had just time to see the Amazon, her beautiful face aflame with fury, before she seized him again, this time by the throat. Whirled from his feet, he was lifted clean over her head and hurtled across the control room as though shot from a gun.

He staggered up just in time to meet a straight right that spun him around so he fell flat on his face. The Amazon did not stop here. Whirling him up with one hand, she used the other to batter him relentlessly in the face.

Relka did not interfere. He had dropped by the control panel and set the course. He watched the proceedings with interest.

"I owed you that, Quorne," the Amazon snapped, her eyes aflame. "Now start explaining how you pulled that trick on me!"

"Apparently you have recovered your strength, Miss Brant," he said, and considering his bad condition, his voice sounded remarkably strong.

"I've done more than that, Quorne: I have you beaten! Now tell me what I want to know before I thrash you still more."

"Simply explained," Quorne responded, breathing hard. "When your *Ultra* crossed the alarm system I turned the telescopes on space and identified your craft. Up to that moment I had lost track of you. I didn't know whether you or the Jovian were flying the vessel—assuming, as I did, that you were still a weakling. Finally I saw you were heading for Pluto— so I got there first by instantaneous transportation, using a space suit for protection. I materialized a little time ahead of you, watched my chance—since I knew approximately where you would land—and then endeavoured to strand you. I can't think why I didn't."

"Because our guide lines carried us with the ship," the Amazon retorted. "Thanks for the explanation— but you outsmarted yourself, Quorne. I'm going to kill you—just as you once said you would kill me."

Quorne grinned enigmatically through his battered lips, then the Amazon snatched out her proton gun and fired it point blank. Sefner Quorne vanished in a momentary flash of unbearable flame and the atomic dust to which he had been reduced floated about the warm air of the control-room.

The Amazon slowly returned her gun to its holster

and then turned. She gave a taut smile.

"Such an unexciting finish I can hardly credit it," she commented musingly, returning to where Relka was standing by the switchboard. "I'm surprised at Quorne being such a fool as to walk right into the danger. He always struck me as being too clever for that."

"The guide lines fooled him," the Jovian pointed out. "He'd have won the day but for that. What happens now? Do we return to Pluto?"

"Yes. We carry on with our original plan. Even the death of Quorne does not alter the fact that those ten brains are still in action—and I do not suppose Quorne's demise will prevent his immediate followers carrying on in his absence."

The Amazon settled at the control board, swung the nose of the *Ultra* slowly around, then began heading back for the remote little world on the rim of the system. As she went she switched on the space radio, and just as she had anticipated, orders and directives were still being poured forth from the Earth's radio transmitters.

"We'll need to wait a while to be sure—there's a considerable time lag in radio reaching us from Earth," the Amazon commented.

More than half an hour passed, and there was no cessation. Obviously the power of Quorne lived on after him, in the hands of capable assistants. As yet these individuals probably did not know what had happened to their leader—which was as the Amazon wanted it. She was prepared for trouble in the future. When Quorne failed to return, avengers might set forth and make things difficult.

* * * * * * *

Once the return to Pluto had been accomplished, the Amazon wasted no time in putting her plans in action. She brought the *Ultra* down close to the high tableland she and Relka had been exploring when they had been snatched away—and this time she took care to lock the machine's controls just in case anything else unexpected happened. Then she and the Jovian, enveloped in their spacesuits, began to unload the machine tools necessary for their task.

Using the *Ultra*'s power plant—diverted for the purpose—the machine tools first fashioned two towers, a mile apart, both of them 1,000 feet in height. It was a task which by old-fashioned standards would have taken years, but the beams and vibrational moulders used by the Amazon fashioned the towers section on section as the hours passed. An endless supply of metal, packed in its tiny atomic form, was fed into the instruments responsible for the job. The atomic metal followed a pre-governed pattern and became normal metal upon reaching its required position. So, gradually, without welding or bolting, the towers climbed— each piece fitting into the other by the unbreakable force of interlocked atomic structures.

It took twelve hours to build each tower. Then came the greater task, to equip each tower with the powerful four-dimensional machinery necessary to deflect the far distant planet out of its orbit.

"You really believe it can be done?" the Jovian questioned.

"The science of mathematics doesn't lie, Relka," the Amazon responded. "It is all a matter of stresses and strains and engineering principles. At the top of each tower will be the necessary equipment for the job. We had to have the towers so the machinery can have a rigid base—and, also to raise us above the neutralizing effect of Pluto's surface, which where four-dimensional mechanics are involved constitutes an earthing circuit. I'm going to the summit while you control things from the ground. You know what to do."

Relka nodded. Every plan had been thoroughly worked out. Then he stood and watched as the Amazon's space-suited figure began the upward climb—a task that was rendered harder by the weight of her suit and the pull of the not inconsiderable gravity.

She rested three times in the ascent then at last scrambled over the edge of the big metal platform that was to house the apparatus. Down below there was only the gleam of light from the *Ultra*: everything else was black, the darkness which eternally blanketed this remote world.

She took the small radio phone from her suit to communicate with Relka below—then she paused, her eyes chained to a curving tail of sparks amidst the spangling stars overhead. Not very far away a spaceship was approaching. And not one, either—but several. In a matter of ten seconds she counted the exhausts of six machines sweeping ever nearer.

"Relka!" she snapped into the suit's internal microphone. "I don't know if trouble is headed this way or not, but some fliers are coming. Get to the *Ultra* and have the guns ready."

She heard his acknowledgement, then she switched off and stood watching the exhaust trails coming nearer, until it occurred to her that she was in a dangerous position. She dropped back over the plate edge, going round the massive girders until the metal above formed a roof.

Then the question of whether friend or foe was coming was resolved as a battery of destructive beams opened up against the tower. It quivered and rocked under the onslaught, the Amazon clinging on desperately to the girders. Around her she saw the metal fusing and dripping under blinding fire as atomic aggregates were ripped asunder by the beams. Now and again she caught a glimpse of the fliers moving like angry wasps, rocket exhausts streaming as they kept the towers in focus.

After a while several girders snapped under the strain and the Amazon felt herself pitching forward as the top of her particular tower crashed sideways as though on a hinge—but the twisted girders still supporting one side of it did not entirely part. She hung on, wondering how long it would be before the summit fell off and dropped her a thousand feet to the rock below.

The neighbouring tower was alight with devouring atomic flame, its whole mass slowly disintegrating under the attack—but now Relka was at work, for the *Ultra*'s deadly weapons were spouting destruction, trapping one spaceship after another in a mesh of vibrations and beams which brought three machines crashing down before they could get clear.

The remainder did not stay to risk annihilation. Their exhaust showed they were speeding rapidly into distance, and, finally, they were lost to sight.

The Amazon stirred, her face grim. Very carefully she eased her body across the trembling mass of twisted metalwork, then gaining what remained of the tower she began a swift descent to the ground. Her first move was to go to the three machines that had been brought down. Finding no external bolts on the airlocks she returned to Relka and with his help carried a disintegrator across the plain and turned its force on the ships' metalwork. In each one a hole was torn, allowing air to explode outward into the vacuum and killing whoever might have been left alive in each vessel.

Silent, the Amazon and Relka stood in the gap of a broken hull and looked at the occupants of the control room. There were three men, already solid and glazed with space-zero, and they were so much alike they might have been triplets. The Amazon considered them for several moments in the light of her torch— then she led the way across the plain to the remaining two shattered vessels. In each of these, also, were three men—identical in every detail with the first three.

Making up her mind about something, she hacked a piece of frozen flesh from the hand of one of the men and took it back with her to the *Ultra*, Relka following behind. When they were in the warmth of the *Ultra*'s laboratory they took off their space suits and the Amazon went to work analyzing the piece of flesh with a series of instruments. When she had finished her yellow face was grim.

"This is synthetic flesh, Relka," she snapped, swinging on him. "All the nine men controlling those machines were not living human beings at all: they were mass-produced from one pattern, the pattern of some man whom Quorne must have decided would make an ideal model for a synthetic man."

"From your mind, Amazon," Relka responded, "I read that you believed synthesis was your secret alone."

"It was! It was one of the mysteries that baffled Abna, and which I never divulged to him. But Quorne has discovered the secret, and I think I know how. It dates back to the time when I duplicated the Archbishop of Canterbury. I know that Quorne discovered a synthetic archbishop was used. He probably analyzed the constitution of that substitute body and by scientific deduction solved the problem. He seems to have also discovered how to make the images obey by imprinting his own orders on their brains."

"But—" The Jovian's thoughts paused as he was plainly bewildered. "How did these beings attack as they did if the guiding genius—Quorne—is dead?"

"I don't believe he is," the Amazon answered slowly. "This new discovery leads me to think that it was not Quorne I attacked and killed—but an image of him. In other words, I fell for the same deception that I have practised on my enemies many a time, when I have used an image of myself and kept my own personality free. Come to think of it," she went on, "Quorne himself hardly would desert Earth and come to Pluto, no matter how urgent the need, because Earth demands his attention every moment if it is to be kept in subjection. With an image, controlled by a long-distance mental wave, he could quite easily attack. He would see all that the image saw by television-connections behind the eyes of the creature, just as he would hear by radio-connections in the ears. I've performed the trick myself scores of times."

"But you held a conversation with him," Relka pointed out. "If you were actually talking to Quorne back on Earth, there'd have been a delay."

The Amazon shook her head impatiently. "Quorne obviously utilized the fourth dimension in such a way that he could communicate almost instantaneously.... If only I had not destroyed the creature whom I took to be Quorne! An analysis would have shown me immediately whether synthesis was used."

"I think," the Jovian commented, after a long interval, "that we may take it for granted that Quorne is still alive—and that he sent those fliers in an effort to destroy your work here. He knows you have some scheme in mind, but is not sure of its nature. All he can do is harass you— What I do not understand is why he didn't destroy you and all your works from Earth with a beam of some kind, as he did on Jupiter."

"There are two possible reasons," the Amazon responded. "Here our distance is vastly greater than on Jupiter—and there are limits to the extent of Quorne's beam projectors: and secondly, he is hampered because on Pluto here there is no light to show our position, and even his telescopes will not be powerful enough to pick up the glow of the *Ultra*'s portholes. On Jupiter he knew the exact position of the dome because he once lived there. He can only attack by direct methods— as he has done—by giving synthetic pilots orders to destroy everything of a scientific nature which they observe—or else he will next attempt to smash us by using four-dimensional tricks which will shorten the distance he has to operate across."

"From the radio and the orders being given out, I fancy we may be certain Quorne lives," Relka commented. "And we can also be sure that he will make every possible move to destroy us or, failing that, blow our plans sky high. So what do we do next?"

"He does not know what is intended and I still think we may take him by surprise," the Amazon responded; "so we continue as before, but with certain precautions. We'll construct a power unit outside, near the *Ultra*, and use it to give off a field of force. That should extend for 2,000 feet around us, which will mean the towers can be rebuilt under a protective but invisible covering. It means a lot of extra work and time, but we must do it."

And, typically, the Amazon wasted no further time talking. She gave Relka his orders and then assisted him to assemble the necessary machine-tool equipment for the making of a subsidiary power plant. To her annoyance forty-eight hours of time were lost in the erection of the plant, set up on the stony waste a few yards from the *Ultra* and powered by the *Ultra*'s own atomic-energy plant. Despite the delay, however, the Amazon considered it had been justified when the plant was set in action and disseminated its curve of force to the required height and distance. It meant that the entire base of operations was shielded by the invisible dome—and it meant also that air could be pumped into the hemisphere and space suits discarded.

Then work began again on the restoration of the towers, a job that was completed without any signs of further attacks from Sefner Quorne. Two weeks passed on Pluto's lonely surface, and by this time the tower platforms were equipped with the complicated, newly made devices necessary for handling the distant planetoid. One tower carried a repulsion beam and the other an attractor beam, both of them operating through a fourth-dimensional angle, the entire engineering feat having been computed from the Amazon's original equations and controlled from a ground level switchboard.

The Amazon said: "We have nothing to do now but try to move the planetoid and then wait the necessary time until it has completed its movements. That, according to my calculations, will be ninety-eight Earth days."

"Which is a long time," the Jovian observed. "Time

in which Sefner Quorne might think of some way of beating us."

The Amazon was silent for a moment. She and the Jovian were in the *Ultra*'s control room, secure here in its warmth and comfort, the shielded instruments and power plant outside governed entirely by remote control from a master matrix.

"So far he hasn't attempted anything," the Amazon said finally. "We'll have to go on taking the risk of attack at any moment. In the meantime our task begins...."

She settled herself more comfortably in the chair before the matrix and her yellow fingers began to play over the varicoloured keys. The power plant hummed more deeply. Outside the slave plant came to life, transferring its power to the equipment at the tower tops. They loomed faintly visible against the stars.

Then the Amazon closed the switches which caused both towers to emit their opposite vibrations simultaneously. A lavender and orange beam stabbed from the tower summits, shading off into nothing as they lost themselves amidst the stars.

Rigid, only too aware of what might happen in the matter of recoil if she made a single mistake, the Amazon moved further keys, gradually bringing into being the four-dimensional circuit. What effect it had on the twin beams was not visible; only the instruments could tell the story—which they did effectually. So far everything was in order. The real work would begin when the vibrations, geared to the distance by compass-reading, struck the infinitely remote planetoid.

"Apparently," Relka said, gazing outside on to the faintly visible beams at the tower tops, "you have removed our energy hemisphere, Amazon? You must have done so to let the beams pass through it—"

"It was the first thing I did," the Amazon responded. "I only hope it wasn't the move Quorne was waiting for, because it leaves us unprotected. Whatever else happens, though, those beams must have free passage."

She turned her attention back to the apparatus, 'feeling' her way through four-dimensional space with the keys. It was a long, exacting task from which she dared not move for a moment—then some two hours later she saw the reaction on the compass needles that revealed the objective had been reached. To cover the huge distance by the fourth dimension had not been so difficult, because the electronic beams had had an initial velocity equivalent to that of light, which was then augmented by the foreshortening of space: it was the task of juggling that strange planetoid towards the solar system that would demand every scientific trick she knew. Even then its initial speed when it entered hyperspace would be much less than that of light— hence her estimate of ninety-eight days before it would arrive.

She settled herself to the job unflinchingly, the Jovian watching in silent interest over her shoulders. It was a decided drawback that the television beams could not be used over the distance, their principle making it impossible for them to be deflected in a fourth dimension. Television in every case relied on straight line principles without the embodiment of curves.

"It's moving," the Amazon murmured after a while, her voice tense. "I'm using a pendulum procedure—first one way, then the other, until finally it should swing over the boundary line and pull free of from its present position. Once that's done half the battle is won...."

Relka made no telepathic comment: he was too afraid of disturbing the Amazon's concentration. As the time passed her fingers became so active on the big keyboard they seemed like a golden mist. Beneath her touch energies came and went, angled back and forth through the fourth dimension, tremendous powers which dragged and then pushed and then dragged that distant planet as though it were a reluctant giant.

The sudden swinging of the needles on three conspicuous meters made the Amazon catch her breath quickly. For a moment she glanced up with triumph in her violet eyes.

"It's moving towards us, Relka! Its gravitational balance has been upset! My figures were correct!"

"And now?" Relka questioned.

"Now I angle it into the fourth dimension. After that I have nothing left to do. It has been given the initial movement that will continue to maintain it on a fixed course. Its path is charted ahead of it, and no other gravitational fields can intervene because the fourth dimension prevents them operating. The next thing we shall have is that alien world appearing at a spot close to Earth in ninety-eight days."

CHAPTER TEN
VICTORY

The throbbing of the power plant died away as the Amazon threw in the cut-out controls. High atop the towers the beams responsible for the four-dimensional miracle wavered and then blanked out. It was as if nothing had ever happened—but somewhere in the Universe, sealed in hyperspace and moving at incredible velocity, was the hell-planetoid, travelling ever nearer on its predestined track to a spot near Earth.

"We'll have a meal and a rest, and then collect our equipment from outside," the Amazon said. "We've done all we can with it."

The Jovian nodded and hurried off to the storage cupboard. He and the Amazon had their meal, slept for a while, and then again prepared for work. The Amazon flung back the massive clamps on the airlock door. Then as she was half over the metal rim to the exterior she stopped, looking into a row of protonic guns projecting straight at her in the flood of light from behind her.

She made an endeavour to jump back and slam the airlock door but she was not quick enough. Three of the figures leaped after her, their guns ready, and their united strength sent her sprawling across the control room to fall in a corner. Relka dived immediately to her assistance only to find himself suddenly pulled up short by manacles about his wrists and ankles. His space suit was ripped from him by the keen edge of a knife, then he was hurled against one of the ceiling struts and there secured immovably.

The Amazon got slowly on her feet, saying nothing as her helmet was opened and her suit taken from her. By this time the airlock was shut again and six men in space suits were within the control room. One of them tugged off his suiting while the remaining five kept their weapons levelled.

It was no surprise to the Amazon when the slender, austere figure of Sefner Quorne became visible. He tossed his spacesuit on one side, smoothed back his ruffled hair, then surveyed her.

"So I was right," she commented. "I did only destroy an image of you."

"Painful though the realization must be to you, Miss Brant—yes," Quorne assented, and gave his cold smile. "I congratulate you on the energy hemisphere with which you surrounded yourself: it kept me entirely at bay. All we could do was land near here and wait until such time as you removed the barrier. The moment you did that we came within it. Even then we had not the equipment with us to penetrate this *Ultra* of yours, so we had to wait until you stepped outside— Then you know what happened."

The Amazon shrugged, cold fury in her eyes. "And now what?"

"I have had a long journey here, Miss Brant. I have delegated my power on Earth to one Nalgo in my absence—but loyal though he is, he may not be able to hold Earth's masses as I can. In other words, I have risked a good deal to come here and accomplish what my image failed to do: destroy you forever, along with this Jovian barbarian whom you seem to have made your friend. I had no other way than personal contact to kill you, so that is my intention. But I must know first just what you have been doing here all these weeks and how much your plans interfere with my own."

"If the positions were reversed, Quorne, I cannot imagine you telling me your plans," the Amazon commented.

"That would depend upon my physical resistance," he said. "I know you are not the kind of woman to hesitate at inflicting the maximum suffering on a victim just as long as you learn all you require. I, too, have the same unsentimental streak."

The Amazon did not speak. She glanced at the guns of the five space-suited men still covering her; then Quorne played with his own gun idly as he resumed talking.

"You have been to a great deal of effort to construct two high towers. Miss Brant—even rebuilding them after my earlier ineffectual attempt to destroy them. I noticed beams projecting from them recently—but I don't understand the reason for them. I am asking you to explain."

"You know me better than that, Quorne."

"Yes." Quorne sighed. "I'm afraid I do. You are a clever woman, Miss Brant—too clever, unfortunately. Ready for every move. You have masked your brain, too, so I cannot read your thoughts and know the purpose of those towers. Yet I still must have the facts, so I can prepare for whatever little scientific trick you have arranged for me."

"This is one trick which will give you no warning, Quorne," the Amazon retorted. "You can kill me—and Relka, too—but it still will not save you. I have broken your hold over Earth, though it may be a little while before that fact becomes apparent."

Quorne considered for some moments, then he said:

"Miss Brant, you can be hurt as much as anyone if certain faculties are destroyed with anguishing slowness. For instance, you might find it unpleasant to be left alive and yet a physical wreck. Let us suppose you became blind and deaf, and were then taken to Earth and released amongst the people. That would be infinitely more terrible to you than death."

The Amazon's features quivered for a moment as she knew the merciless danger that threatened, but she did not speak. Quorne's expression changed, then he signalled to four of his men.

Against their strength the Amazon stood no chance, hard though she struggled. She finished up on the long testing table at the far end of the control room, her arms pulled taut to either side of her and secured by the wrists under the table. Remembering past experience, the men used wire, adding more round her ankles and waist for extra security.

Quorne said: "If you tell me now what I wish to know, Miss Brant, I will grant you a quick and merciful death. If you do not, I will learn the facts just the same, but inflict on you an agony that will last you all the days of your almost eternal life. Such is the measure of my hatred for you."

The Amazon stared back at him.

"Whatever you may do, Quorne, you can never make me speak," she answered. "I set myself to destroy you and all your works, and I shan't spoil it now by telling you what I have done."

"As you will," Quorne shrugged, and he turned to the bench.

The Amazon lay watching him. He spent a few moments rigging up a tripod stand with twin lenses, behind which he screwed high-intensity cold-light globes. Throwing a switch, he considered the two brilliant spots of light that cast down on the bench. Then he switched off and moved the tripod so its legs stood over the Amazon's motionless figure. She set her mouth as she saw Quorne adjusting the lenses to pin-point focus. Finally he seized her mass of hair, drew it back in one of his hands, then passed a wire round it. Secured, it held her head immovable.

"I meant every word of my threat, Miss Brant," he stated, looking down on her in cold fury. "You can save yourself—if you wish."

"For death? No, Quorne."

He nodded and from the bench took a roll of sticky-tape. In a matter of seconds the Amazon found her eyelashes gummed back so she could not close her eyelids. The fiendish plan hammered into her brain. Unable to help herself, she would be compelled to stare into those relentless, blazing lenses until all sight had gone.

A crash twirled Quorne round in surprise. He was in time to see Relka tear his powerful arms free of the support to which he had been manacled. Indeed his wrists were still secured, but the tethering chain had snapped. With demonical force he swung his mighty paws down, battering them on the helmets of the space-suited men nearest him. The impact did not stun them, protected as they were, but it sent them stumbling.

This was all Relka needed. He wrenched free of the remaining chain and forced his arms apart. His wrists flew asunder. Protonic guns blazed at him, but he didn't take the slightest notice of them. His armoured skin prevented any real injury.

Seizing the guard nearest to him he swept him into the air, whirled him around, then dashed him with killing force against the wall. Thus far he got when the four remaining men plunged on top of him. Quorne stood watching, realizing his gun was useless. Then he stole across to the giant proton gun used by the Amazon as a defensive weapon.

She for her part, pinned immovably, could only stare at the still dead lenses above her. Her eyes were already smarting intolerably through inability to blink. Concussions reached her ears, the grunts of the men, the savage breathing of Relka as, his helmet removed, he sucked in air through his snarling jaws.

One man attacking Relka crumpled with a broken spine. The second flew through the air, propelled by an arm like a piston rod. The remaining two clung frantically to the mad Jovian's block-like legs, until he kicked them, sending them stunned across the metal floor.

Then the yellow eyes switched to Quorne. He was standing behind the big proton gun and he pressed the release button. But nothing happened. He was not aware that the whole energy of the power plant, which also controlled the gun, was still being diverted to the equipment outside. Relka dived at him. With a violent twisting motion of his body, Quorne avoided the rush and Relka collided heavily with the wall. Then Quorne rushed to the airlock and whirled it open, plunging out wildly into the airless void. Instantly the pressure in the control room began to fall. Relka flew across the floor, slammed the door shut, and then turned the air gauge controls to maximum. Breathing hard, he moved over to where the Amazon still lay pinned. As he pulled the gum strips from her lashes, she lay blinking furiously and waiting while he freed her tethered hair and limbs.

She sat up and Relka looked at her for a moment, then hurried to the porthole, and saw a fiery trail whirling upward to the stars.

"He escaped!" came his amazed thoughts. "He must

have survived the vacuum."

"It can be done, at the expense of a bleeding nose," the Amazon responded. "I've done it myself before now. Bodily warmth is retained for a few seconds in a vacuum because space is an insulator of heat—and you can't burst apart if you expel all air from your lungs for the few seconds you're in sheer space. Trust Quorne to know every trick."

"We have to follow him—" the Jovian began, but the Amazon cut him short.

"Can't do that, Relka. Our power plant has to be converted back to normal before we can even move. All we can do is keep him in the telescopic sights and try and follow him later. You do that while I straighten things out."

She redonned a spacesuit and got rid of the dead guards' bodies through the airlock. Then she went outside and cut the *Ultra* free of the subsidiary power plants it had been operating.

Then she started to restore the central power plant to normal. "Where's Quorne now?"

"Heading back towards home as far as I can tell; he's some millions of miles from Neptune at the moment."

The Amazon nodded. "We'll catch him up quickly enough once we start."

Then she set to work on the power plant, removing connections and replacing others. The delay it caused irritated her, but it had to be done—and without any mistakes. A single false connection might make all the difference between life and death once the journey through space began.

Altogether her task took three hours, by which time Quorne was beginning to fade from view on the reflector screen. Going over to the Jovian's side the Amazon peered at the tiny silvery ovoid moving against the stars, slowly approaching the rim of distant Neptune.

"We'll catch him," she said confidently. "Keep him in the mirror, Relka, and be prepared for plenty of strain from acceleration."

She settled at the control panel and switched on the power plant. It responded instantly, charged to the limit with a new block of copper. Then she advanced the power-control. With a slight jolt the *Ultra* rose, rear rockets flaring for the initial take-off. Easily as a bird the machine swept from the plain, cleared the low mountain ranges, then moved almost vertically upwards towards the stars.

Another notch clicked on the power scale. Then another. The rockets cut out and sheer atomic force repulsion took their place. Building speed on speed the Amazon hurtled the *Ultra* onwards, turning the vessel's nose in a giant arc so that at last she was looking directly ahead toward Neptune—visible at the moment as a round green ball a vast distance ahead.

"He's gone past Neptune," Relka said, watching the screen. "Well on his way to the orbit of Uranus."

The Amazon nodded but did not speak. The velocity of the *Ultra* was increasing with every second as Pluto's grip weakened and Neptune's became apparent.

Fast though Quorne was moving, he could not hope to equal the terrific speed of the *Ultra* under full power.

The springs in the seats holding the Amazon and Relka began to twang presently as their occupants were crushed down under the weight of acceleration. Both of them found their breathing was becoming difficult, and pressure began to build up behind their eyes—but not for a moment did the Amazon relax. Her whole being was concentrated on overtaking Quorne and smashing him for all time.

Neptune's orbit was reached, but the planet itself so far away that no course corrections were needed to combat its gravity. Then the Amazon swung inwards again in the direction of distant Uranus, this time using its gravity field to achieve a slingshot effect and increase her speed still further. The *Ultra* was moving at a pace now which made it necessary for her to rest her arms in specially devised metal clamps, so intensely heavy were they. She refrained from speaking, the weight of her jaws making it difficult to form the words.

Quorne's distant machine began to become visible to her naked eyes as the *Ultra* streaked through infinity in pursuit. It seemed pretty evident that Quorne was giving his flyer the limit of its power, for he did not succeed in increasing his distance from the overtaking *Ultra*. Even so, there were still millions of miles to go and many hours must pass, so the Amazon snapped in the automatic controls and dragged herself out of the control seat.

The tremendous weight of her body nearly flattened

her on the metal floor for a moment; then she just managed to reach the wall couch and fall hard upon it. In this position the strain on her heart and lungs was eased somewhat.

Relka, thanks to his different physical construction and accustomedness to Jovian gravity, was not in such bad shape. With his customary dogged immobility he sat at the mirror, fingering the controls with his scaly paws, keeping that speck of silver constantly in focus.

Minutes drifted into hours. The Amazon slept a little and awoke again to realize that Relka was shaking her quickly.

"He's turning off—heading for Saturn," he said. "We're not very far from him now—or Saturn, either. Obviously he knows he can never reach Earth without you overtaking him, so he's risking moving aside."

With an effort the Amazon struggled up from the couch. During her sleep the *Ultra* had built up even more velocity, had covered the yawning millions of miles in record time. She closed the switch that cut out the acceleration and instantly the crushing weight ceased as constant velocity was achieved. Uranus was far behind. Ahead was magnificent Saturn, his rings tilted to an angle, the dim speck of Quorne's machine looming black against Saturn's cloud-belted disc.

"Do you intend to follow him down there?" Relka questioned.

"Certainly I do." The Amazon watched intently. "I don't know anything about Saturn's surface, chiefly because I've had no reason to try to find out. I assume it will be pretty much like Jupiter's—frozen, with a poisonous atmosphere."

She said no more. The time had come to slow down the *Ultra*'s incredible velocity as the outmost ring of Saturn loomed close. As she had expected, the Amazon suddenly found the *Ultra* involved in a conflicting maze of gravitational fields as the rings, made up of multi-millions of infinitely small moons, added their own attraction to that of the parent body.

The real trouble came when the *Ultra* arrived in the outmost ring itself. It seemed to the two in the control room that the machine was speeding through a snowstorm of shifting, whirling bodies—a state of affairs which, but for the *Ultra*'s repulsive screens and armoured hull, would have smashed it to pieces.

The weird effect lasted for nearly an hour—then the 12,000-mile width of the outer ring was covered and the *Ultra* leapt through Cassini's division—the black emptiness between rings, and sped across its 1,800-mile width.

Then onwards again into the 17,000-mile broadest ring, all sign of Quorne lost now in the whirling brilliance of the pocket moons through which the *Ultra* dodged and twisted and turned like a super-fast submarine moving through a minefield. Then at last the *Ultra* was clear and 8,000 miles distant loomed the rolling cloud belts of Saturn himself.

"There's Quorne!" came Relka's thoughts abruptly, and his scaly finger pointed to a black speck just disappearing in the cloud belts.

The Amazon gave a taut nod, plunged the *Ultra* downward, and then switched on the infra-screens as the machine became enveloped in the swirling density of Saturn's atmosphere. The screens penetrated the obliterating fog effectually and revealed below a scene that held the Amazon and Relka with its inexplicable beauty.

Both the Amazon and the Jovian, knowing the frozen condition of the outer worlds, had been expecting a rugged terrain, but instead they saw a deep-green landscape and the silver threads of rivers. For some obscure reason the entire landscape was flooded with golden light. Since it could not come from the sun, the explanation was hard to conceive. Her brows knitted, the Amazon stared in wonder at the view as the *Ultra* still dropped downward—then as the machine dropped below the cloud-belts she found the screens had not been lying. The glory did exist in every direction. Saturn was a planet of sheer natural beauty in every sense, the golden light flooding down from a mysteriously supported amber-coloured ball of flame just below the cloud-blanket. The Amazon suspected magnetism as the solution, but could not be sure.

Then it occurred to her that Quorne had disappeared. She kept the *Ultra* flying at about 500 feet over the lush valleys and fields, visibility extending as far as her eyes could see, but Quorne had completely disappeared.

"Something queer about this planet, Relka," she muttered. "The most perfect world ever seen—even surpassing Earth in its richness of natural beauty, yet nowhere a sign of life. Such a world as this ought not, by all scientific standards, to exist at all in this part of the system. And yet it does.... As for Quorne, I can't imagine what has become of him."

"Perhaps he dodged back into the cloud-banks?" Relka suggested.

"I think not. We have had the screen penetrating the clouds, and down here we can see to infinity. No—there's some other reason, but I can't think what it is—"

She broke off and stared fixedly ahead. Catching her astounded thoughts, Relka looked, too. They were approaching a city. It gleamed with an iridescent purple in the golden light, its glittering towers reaching up to the cloudbanks, its terraces and streets and magnificent flower gardens all laid out with artistic precision. An amethyst city, in the midst of a wonder world, on a planet that should, by its position, have been frozen and poisonous.

The Amazon could not believe it. She closed her eyes for a moment, then opened them again—and the wonder world had gone! The *Ultra* was instead battling through a hurricane of raging vapours, above a plain of murderous rock.

"I don't understand it," Relka observed, astounded. "Everything has just snapped out, as though it never existed—yet I am convinced it did!"

"It did," the Amazon agreed, "but at the moment we have the conditions we expected—a world of smother and confusion and danger. As for Quorne, we've lost him completely."

She operated the controls quickly, lifting the *Ultra* diagonally from the curiously transformed plain and up into the teeth of the howling winds and poison gases... until at last she had driven clear of the atmospheric belt and was back in space with the 'minefield' of pocket-moons ahead.

"Well?" Relka questioned.

"Of all the worlds I have visited and seen none has been the equal of Saturn," the Amazon answered, locking down on it broodingly. "A world of inexplicable mystery, which somehow has swallowed up my most dangerous enemy. Whether he is dead or not I do not know.... At least I don't think he will come back to Earth. Once that hell-planetoid materialises, we can free Earth and then perhaps find out what really exists on Saturn here. I've got to know: it's too scientifically wonderful to miss. And I must also know what happened to Quorne. As long as his fate is in doubt, he remains the greatest menace in the Universe."

She said no more, swinging the great vessel around and then forward, in readiness for its battle with the rings.

* * * * * * *

The Amazon did not return to Earth. Once she had brought the *Ultra* safely through the moons of Saturn she headed to a point some 20,000 miles from the spot where calculations had shown her the hell planetoid would materialize; then, with Relka, she prepared to wait for its coming. It also enabled her to keep a constant watch on space in case Quorne showed signs of returning.

But nothing happened. The spaceways remained dead, and far away in the void Saturn gleamed in lonely splendour, her secret masked under the everlasting clouds. From Earth, via radio, there came evidence that the ten-brain equipment was still functioning, presumably under the directions of Nalgo, Quorne's right-hand man.

Until, three months later, the hell planet from furthest space made its appearance out of the fourth dimension 20,000 miles away from where the *Ultra* was motionless. It came first as a transparent circle, then as a gradually solidifying globe catching the light of the sun. Inevitably its gravity produced shifts and changes. The world's oceans rocked as floating balls in water might do when a heavy body drops amongst them, but the effect quickly lessened as a new balance was struck.

The outflowing waves of hypnosis from Earth were blocked and reflected back by the strange semi-sentient planet with devastating results. In a matter of hours the Earth radios and television were screaming the news that hypnosis was destroyed, that the ten-brain amplifier had been blown out of the casing in which it had been housed. The people were freed, and wondering about the presence of a small new moon in the skies of Earth.

Above all, where was the Golden Amazon? Where

was Abna?

The Amazon smiled a little as she switched off the radio. She glanced at Relka.

"The job's done, my friend," she said. "We've added a second moon to Earth and destroyed this particular phase of Quorne's activities. To return to Earth and get things in order again will he simple. As for Abna...."

The Amazon looked away toward distant Jupiter for a while, her yellow face expressionless: then she looked beyond Jupiter to the world next in order, Saturn.

She thought of the landscape of incomparable beauty, the amethyst city, and then Sefner Quorne. Somehow—someday—she had to know.

She closed the power-switches and the *Ultra* turned toward the liberated Earth.

ABOUT THE AUTHOR

British writer JOHN RUSSELL FEARN was born near Manchester, England, in 1908. As a child he devoured the science fiction of Wells and Verne, and was a voracious reader of the Boys' Story Papers. He was also fascinated by the cinema, and first broke into print in 1931 with a series of articles in *Film Weekly*.

He then quickly sold his first novel, *The Intelligence Gigantic*, to the American magazine, *Amazing Stories*. Over the next fifteen years, writing under several pseudonyms, Fearn became one of the most prolific contributors to all of the leading US science fiction pulps, including such legendary publications as *Astounding Stories*, *Startling Stories*, *Thrilling Wonder Stories*, and *Weird Tales*.

During the late 1940s he diversified into writing novels for the UK market, and also created his famous superwoman character, The Golden Amazon, for the prestigious Canadian magazine, the Toronto *Star Weekly*. In the early 1950s in the UK, his fifty-two novels as "Vargo Statten" were bestsellers, most notably his novelization of the film, *Creature from the Black Lagoon*.

Apart from science fiction, he had equal success with westerns, romances, and detective fiction, writing an amazing total of 180 novels—most of them in a period of just ten years—before his early death in 1960. His work has been translated into nine languages, and continues to be reprinted and read worldwide.

www.ingramcontent.com/pod-product-compliance
Lightning Source LLC
Chambersburg PA
CBHW050732250626
47155CB00005B/1761